PAPA DON'T PREACH

Sade C. Morrison

Acknowledgements

I am grateful to God first and foremost for all of His abundant blessings. Thanks to my family and friends who encouraged me to write. I would also like to extend a special thanks to my editor, Linda Turner. Last but not least, I truly appreciate my readers. I am so humbled by your support. You inspire me to tell stories from my heart.

Jackie

ONE

According to my father's wisdom, demons were to blame for all of my missteps. If Daddy found out about my latest crisis, I'm sure he'd advise me in his commanding baritone to *"Come back to the Lord's house and He can make everything all right!"* But Daddy's Christian faith had not spared him from sorrow, so I doubted that attending church would solve my dilemma.

Daddy spoke of demons as if they were computer-generated creatures that could be zapped away by some hero with a holy sword. I thought back to my childhood Sundays at New Kingdom Baptist Church. I used to sit in the third pew, wearing a starched dress, stockings and patent-leather shoes, my hair neatly plaited and adorned with colorful ribbons and barrettes.

My heartbeat always quickened when Daddy preached about demons. I feared they were hiding under floorboards, lurking behind toilet stalls and whispering inside of hissing radiators. But life had taught me that the most difficult demons to cast aside were internal.

The past two weeks had been a combination of depressing days and hectic ones. The moment my personal life took an unpredictable turn, my job became my religion. In the past thirteen days, I'd put hundreds of miles on my car freelancing as a wedding photographer from Toledo, Ohio to Midland, Michigan. Those gigs and my day job at Center Stage Studios kept me too busy to face my new reality.

Today was the calmest day I'd had since everything changed. I closed my eyes as I submerged my toes into the hot, sudsy water. I tried my best not to think about my situation or speculate about my father's opinion of it. Although I hadn't spoken to the man in nearly a month, he was still a constant presence in my mind (despite my efforts to pretend I didn't care about what he thought.)

"How are you today, miss?" Jung asked in her Korean, singsong accent.

"Fine." I sighed.

She massaged my weary feet. "You seem stressed."

"I'm okay."

"Is your friend coming today?"

"I hope so."

Ten minutes later, I heard a familiar voice. "Hey, Jackie!"

I opened my eyes to the sight of Diane making her way across the busy nail salon. She was a plump, brown-skinned woman with "sister-girl hips" and an infectious smile.

"Hey, girl!" I waved at her.

"Sorry I'm late. Byron had a touch of diarrhea this morning. I tried to explain to him that little tummies get very angry when they skip their vegetables for dinner and eat three Pop-Tarts in the morning. And the worst part of it is that they were chocolate chip. I didn't even know Pop-Tarts came in *chocolate chip*. Maybe if they had been strawberry, it wouldn't have been so bad. But I doubt they put real fruit in 'em anyway. I have a feeling he snuck them into the shopping cart when I wasn't paying attention. Or maybe...maybe Tommy bought them when he went shopping last week. Goodness knows we can't have that junk in our house–"

"Relax. You're here now, all is forgiven." I didn't want to hear another word about her youngest son's eating *or* bathroom habits. Diane had a tendency to bore me with the details of her blended family, which she referred to as the "Mocha Brady Bunch." When she and Tommy got hitched, she had a teenage daughter and he had three sons from a previous marriage. Ten months into their union, Byron was born (the surprise bundle of joy she affectionately calls their "oopsy baby.") Now, Diane was mama to a tribe of five children ranging from a kindergartener to a college senior.

I didn't know the first thing about motherhood or matrimony. Instead of kids and a husband, I had life experiences that were the makings of a bestselling memoir.

At my dream job for *Soul Beat,* I did photo shoots for the who's who of black entertainment from Aretha Franklin to Alicia Keys. I also traveled to locations like Paris and Cape Town to capture special events on film. I was one of the most renowned photojournalists at the magazine, and I had the accolades, the immaculate Manhattan condo and the cute little black BMW to show for it.

Although Mr. Right eluded me, my career provided all the fulfillment I needed. My longest relationship lasted for eight years with JC Bennett, a jazz musician who scored soundtracks for the likes of Spike Lee and Martin Scorsese. We were a power couple in the Harlem arts community. But we split up on the night I opened my closet door to a scantily clad Brazilian model who he claimed was "just a friend."

After I dumped JC, I channeled my pain into my work. During the Great Recession, my portfolio of award-winning photos enabled me to hold on to my job while many of my colleagues were handed pink slips. But my talents did not shield me from the industry-wide shift from print to digital. As publications traded thick magazine spreads for online blogs, the need for photographers like me diminished. A few months after I was laid off, my condo went into foreclosure. I searched for jobs everywhere and the only one I could find was at Center Stage Studios in Detroit.

I had never planned to come back home, but when Daddy picked me up at the airport, he greeted me with a hug and said, *"Man plans and God laughs, sweetheart."* That was four years ago. While the Motor City lacks the amenities I grew accustomed to in New York, living downtown is a far cry from the now-desolate east side neighborhood where I grew up. I managed to find all of my creature comforts from Pad Thai to organic produce. I even found a man who fit most of my criteria. I was relatively happy until about two weeks ago.

"You can sit there." Jung's voice brought me back to my miserable present. She pointed to the empty pedicure chair next to me.

Dianne took off her sneakers and socks and plopped down in the chair. Under the florescent lights, the bags under her eyes looked more pronounced than usual. Her dark hair was brushed back into a tight ponytail. At the nape of her neck, I could see the tight coils revealing her natural hair texture.

Years ago, she used to go to the salon every other Friday. Diane always turned heads with her En Vogue-inspired dos and glamorous makeup. These days, her family obligations kept her so busy that she rarely had time to do anything for herself. Even a Saturday afternoon pedi had to be scheduled around the kids' extracurricular activities and Tommy's factory shifts.

Diane dipped her feet into the water and took a very deep breath. "This is just what I needed."

"I heard that!"

"So how are you holding up?"

"Work is fine."

"I'm not talking about work."

"We're not going to discuss *that* today."

"I know something that will cheer you up." Her amber eyes lit up the same way they did thirty-four years ago when we sat next to each other in English Literature class at Cass Technical High School and she knew the answer to Mrs. Levine's question about Ernest Hemingway.

"What?"

"On Wednesday night, the church is launching our fitness ministry program, 'Prayer, Sweat and Fellowship.' Lord knows I could use it. I've tried just about everything to get rid of this spare tire."

"*Prayer, Sweat and Fellowship?* Who came up with that name?" I smiled.

"The Women's Committee."

"Aren't you on that committee?"

"Do you have a point?"

I chuckled. "It's just a silly name. But I guess it could be worse...like *Pray the Fat Away.*"

"Well, I think it's a worthy mission. All of God's people should strive for good health. Besides, you just might meet a man who loves the Lord and looks good in his workout clothes."

"Please don't go there. It's only been two weeks since..."

"I know you're hurting, girl. But Patrick wasn't the

one for you anyway."

"Because he didn't marry me?"

"That's one reason."

"I know I'll never convince you that a happy relationship can exist outside of matrimony, but it does happen! I was completely content with my Oprah/ Stedman situation."

"Even those times when he didn't come home until three in the morning?"

"So you're telling me that wives are immune from infidelity?"

"That's not what I–"

"Patrick stepped out a few times, but at least he was never sloppy about it. He never brought it to my doorstep until..."

"You deserve better."

"As in a man who doesn't cheat? Then I guess I'm destined to die alone."

"I'm gonna pray for you, girl."

"I appreciate that, but please don't feel sorry for me. I've really thought this out. Patrick had his flaws, but overall, we were good together. I did everything within reason to make my relationship work. I cooked gourmet meals four times a week, I washed his dirty drawers and I went to three Thanksgivings in a row at his mother's house and got parched from her bone-dry turkey."

Diane smiled. "Yeah, girl, my heart went out to you every November. But when you said you did everything within reason, you left out the most important thing. Your relationship had no spiritual base."

"I know how you feel about me and Patrick 'living in sin,' but I can't picture getting married before I'm sure that my husband and I are compatible in the bedroom."

"Tommy and I waited."

"Come on, girl, it's not like you were a virgin on your wedding night. Back in the day, we used to hang at all the clubs."

"But you know all of that changed when I met Tommy. When you love the Lord and you truly love the man you're with, you can give up anything."

"So you don't miss it at all? Never?"

"What's there to miss? Drinking until I had a hangover or waiting by the phone for some man that I gave the most precious piece of myself to decide if he's going to call me? I'm just grateful that God spared me from catching a disease that could have ended my life. And it's true that Tommy and I weren't virgins when we met, but we both waited for each other. And as you know, Tommy and I have a blessed union and we are compatible in all ways."

"That's obvious. Bryon is the flesh and blood proof of just how much y'all love each other."

She grinned.

"But you got lucky. I'm pretty sure that I would end up with a dud in stud's clothing on my honeymoon."

"Tommy and I weren't lucky, we were blessed. When

God sends you the right partner, you have nothing to worry about."

Jung finished filling my toenails. "Go pick a color now."

"Thank you." I glanced at my feet. They looked and felt brand new. I slipped into my pedicure sandals and hurried across the room to the rack of nail polishes. Although I loved Diane like a sister, I was happy to have a temporary reprieve from her point of view. Most of the times, I thought she was too entrenched in her Christianity to acknowledge human emotions like weakness and temptation. But there was a small part of me that was uncomfortable because I wondered if she was right.

I picked up a brownish red shade with subtle sparkles. It was just my style, dramatic and classy. I showed it to Diane and Jung.

Jung looked up from massaging Diane's feet. "That's a very pretty color, miss."

"Mmmhmm, I think I want that one too."

I sat down in the pedicure chair.

"So, on another topic, what are you gonna do for your fiftieth?" Diane asked.

"Seeing as how I can still pass for thirty-eight, I don't see the point of obsessing about it."

"Did your AARP card come in the mail yet?"

"No!" I shook my head. It was a milestone that scared me, especially since I was facing it alone. I was a single woman with severed family ties. Besides Diane and a few associates at work, I didn't have any real friends. All of my New York buddies stopped returning my phone calls when I came to the Midwest. In five decades of living, I couldn't even fill a restaurant booth with people who truly loved me.

"When I turned fifty, I felt so blessed to have lived for half of a century that I prayed for half a century more."

"You really want to live to be one-hundred? I'd hate to imagine how shriveled up and wrinkled up I'd be at that age."

"There must be plenty of advantages. You get to meet all of your great-grandchildren and maybe some great-great-grandkids too. On top of that, if a bill collector calls, you can just say, something like…" She mimicked an old woman. *"Now Sonny, I've been paying on this here Visa since before Noah built the arc. Could you please find it in your heart to forgive this debt?"*

I laughed. "I doubt that would work."

"Sure it will." She chuckled. "But seriously, how do you want to do to celebrate the big 5-0?"

"You know I'm not into big parties. Before this whole thing blew up with Patrick, he was going to take me to Hawaii. If only we could have stayed together for a few more weeks, I would have gotten a great trip out of it."

My cell phone rang. I unzipped my purse and looked at the screen. It was a number I didn't recognize, but the caller had a local 313 area code. I decided to answer it, hoping it was a new client. "Hello, Jacqueline Foster speaking."

I heard static.

"Hello?"

More static.

"Please call me back, I can't hear you."

"Jackie!" A frantic female voice hollered.

"Who is this?"

"Jackie, it's Rhonda!"

I hung up the phone. Whenever she called, it was usually to "borrow" money, but I wasn't in the mood to hear her pathological lies. Rhonda's drug addiction ravaged her youth and beauty so severely that strangers believed *she* was the older sister, despite the fact that I was over a decade her senior. As much as I loved her and missed her, I wanted nothing to do with Rhonda in her current state.

"Who was it?"

"Oh, just a telemarketer."

"I hate when they call. Nowadays, they bother you on the weekends and even as late a nine o'clock. That's why I don't answer the phone if I don't recognize the number."

"I'll be taking that advice from now on."

Rhonda

TWO

The corns on my feet burned. My mouth was dry. I felt like crying, but I didn't want the attention. If I had an emotional break down in the middle of the sidewalk, I figured nobody would bother to ask me, *"Are you all right?"* Instead of showing concern for a person in need, folks would call 911, *"There's a crazy lady on the corner of Joy and Dexter!"*

I wasted my whole afternoon looking for a pay phone. I checked the parking lots of liquor stores, party stores, dollar stores and gas stations. After two hours, I found one that worked. It had bubblegum stuck on the spot where I was supposed to put my ear.

So nasty! What makes somebody do a thing like that anyway? I fetched two quarters out of my pocket (my last bit of cash) and stuck them into the coin slot. I punched Jackie's number and held the phone up close enough for me to hear, but far away enough so that my skin wouldn't touch the used gum.

While I listened to the phone ringing, I looked around the phone booth and read all the bad words people scratched into the glass. It's a shame their parents didn't raise them right because Daddy taught me to never use foul language and I couldn't dream of writing curse words in a public place.

"Hello, Jacqueline Foster speaking," she answered in a professional voice. But then again, Jackie always had a gift for communicating. When we were kids, I told her that she belonged on the radio, but the only thing she ever wanted to do was take pictures of everyone *and* everything with her Nikon camera. I was so jealous of the attention she gave it over me, her adorable little sister. But looking back, I think my life would have turned out better if I would have found something I was passionate about besides Nate.

"Jackie, it's me."

"Hello?"

"Jackie!"

"Please call me back, I can't hear you."

I shouted her name as loud as I could.

"Who is this?"

"Jackie, it's Rhonda!"

Silence. I knew she heard me, but I also knew that she probably didn't want to talk to me. I kept on repeating her name anyway, praying with every breath she might have a change of heart. Last month, I borrowed six hundred dollars from Jackie to keep my heat from getting turned off.

I promised I would find a job and pay it back. Neither one of those things happened. I ended up using two hundred dollars to set up a payment plan with DTE. I bought a few groceries. I was doing just fine until my son's birthday.

I started to think about how nice it would be to bake a big cake for Antoine and watch him blow out all nine candles. The picture in my head made me cry. It's been two years since I've seen Antoine because the judge gave my ex full custody of him. Even though Nate and I used to get high *together,* he convinced the judge that I was the only "unfit" parent. But everybody believes his lies. He's a functioning addict who shows up to work on time and sings in the church choir all while snorting cocaine throughout the day.

I miss my kids. I know Nate won't let me come around Antoine and my daughter, Jaimaya doesn't want anything to do with me. She's grown now (or at least she thinks she is at nineteen years old.) The last time I saw her, my heart broke when she said, "You don't deserve to call yourself a mother!"

The more I thought about my life and how messed up it was, the worse I felt. Those bad feelings spread over my whole body and I went looking for a cure. It worked for a few days. But when the high wore off, I was angry at myself for blowing the rest of Jackie's loan on my bad habit.

A few weeks later, a man in a white van came and shut off my heat *and* my electricity. My friend gave me a kerosene lamp. I lived in the house like that for as long as I could, but March was almost as cold as February, so I moved into a shelter. I thought about going back to Daddy's, but I was too ashamed. I know it would break his heart to see me now.

I don't even like looking at myself anymore. Whenever I walk past a mirror, I turn away. I even brush my teeth with my eyes closed. But I used to love my reflection. I was pretty, just like Jackie. We have the same chocolate brown eyes (from Daddy) and full lips (from Mama.) My flawless, hazelnut complexion used to be the stuff of skincare commercials and my smile was so perfect that people used to ask me if I'd ever had braces. And my naturally long, wavy hair was my crowning glory.

Now, my face is covered with pockmarks and dark blemishes. I am missing six teeth, three in the back of my mouth and three in the bottom front. My only saving grace is that if I smile a certain way, it's not so obvious. My hair is brittle and stringy, some of it is so long that it still falls down my back and the rest is uneven. Most the hair I have left is light brown, but I get more silver strands every day.

But the worst side effect of my addiction is my weight loss. I once had a nice, curvy shape and a wardrobe of clothes to flaunt it. I never dressed in anything revealing, (Daddy wasn't having it) but I was always cute and fashionable. Now, I doubt if I tip the scales at ninety pounds.

I carry around a picture of what I used to look like before I made a choice that ruined my life. If I start feeling depressed, (which happens a lot) I take it out of my pocket and stare at it and say, "Rhonda, I know you're still in there somewhere. With the Lord's strength, I'm going to find you and never let you slip away again." The mission to keep that promise has had its share of setbacks, but I won't stop trying. Daddy raised me to never give up.

I shouted Jackie's name over and over again. After a few seconds of silence, I heard a dial tone. I slammed the pay phone receiver down. A cold wind blew. I shivered a little. It was the first week of spring, but it felt like November. It was a cloudy day of about forty degrees, with a wind-chill of thirty. I always wanted to leave Detroit and go to California. I love beaches. But I never got myself together enough to make it out of Michigan.

I wore a pair of sweat pants, a t-shirt that's been washed so many times I couldn't read the letters anymore and a thin jacket that was two sizes too big. All of my clothes were donated to me. It's been so long since I've been shopping for something new the way Daddy used to take us to Hudson's for Easter dresses. I always picked a pink one. I love pink, it's a color that makes me remember happy times like hunting on the church grounds for rainbow-colored Easter eggs and unwrapping the gold foil on a chocolate bunny.

Thinking about food made my stomach grumble. I made my way across the street to Big Mike's Coney Island. With every painful step, I fantasized about chili fries, a hamburger and a large Coke. Since I spent my last fifty cents calling Jackie, I was broke. My only option was to do something I hated to get some money.

I stood a few feet away from the restaurant entrance and held up my sign that read: *"I'm Hungry. I Pray You Will Help Me."*

A young woman pulled up in a new, gray Ford Explorer. As she got out of the car, the sun peaked through the clouds. I looked up to heaven, hoping that she will put a few coins in my empty Styrofoam cup.

"Excuse me, miss, do you think you could spare some change?"

She hurried inside without saying a word to me. I might as well have been invisible. She could have at least looked me in the eye like a human being and said, "I'm sorry, I can't help you out today."

I blinked away a tear. When people ignored me, it hurt more than anything.

A man in a souped-up classic Camaro parked in the space closest to me. When he got out of the car, I cleared my throat and said, "Excuse me, sir…"

He grinned and reached into his back pocket. He took out two twenty-dollar bills and approached me. "How about if I give you this and buy you something to eat."

I smiled. "That would be a blessing, sir."

"We can make that happen if you take a li'l ride with me…"

I frowned.

"Don't worry, we won't go too far. We'll just pick a quiet spot where we can be alone and you can take care of a brotha's needs."

I took a step back. My drug addiction had brought me face-to-face with many men like him, but I had never crossed the line into prostitution. The times when I was so high and out of it that I almost gave in, Mama whispered in my ear for me to walk away and I always did. I could hear her voice clearly, even though she was all the way up in heaven.

"I'm not like that!" I shouted. "You got it all wrong! Leave me alone!"

He took a step toward me and grinned. "You a li'l feisty thing, ain't you? What if I double my offer?"

"No!" I took another step back and felt my body collide with someone else's. When I turned around, a heavy-set Middle Eastern man in an apron was standing there.

"I'm so sorry, sir, I didn't mean to–"

"You cannot do that sort of thing here," the man said in a thick Arabic accent.

The man who propositioned me walked inside of the restaurant with a smirk on his face.

"Sir, I'm just hungry. I didn't mean to cause any

trouble. I would never–"

"I tell you what, come in, have something to eat and then you leave, okay?"

I nodded as I followed him inside. The heat warmed my body.

"What you want to eat?"

"It doesn't matter. I'm not picky, I'm just hungry."

"Hot dog with french fries, okay?"

I smiled. "Yeah."

"What to drink?"

"Coke, if you have it. I really appreciate this, sir. Thank you so much."

"I do this nice thing for you, then you have to leave. If you no leave, I call police."

"You won't have to do that, sir. I'll leave as soon as I eat."

He walked back toward the kitchen. A few minutes later, he came back out with a tray of food for me. I ate heartily. It was the first real meal I'd had in four days. I tried to take my time and enjoy every bite, but I was so hungry that I could barely taste it. I probably could have eaten anything and my stomach would have been glad.

As I sipped the last of my Coke, the Middle Eastern man came back to me. "Was it good?"

"Yes, sir. Thank you so much."

"You're welcome."

"I'll never forget your kindness. When I get back on my feet, I plan to come back and *buy* my dinner."

"That would be very nice." He paused. "Why are you in the streets this way? Where is your family?"

"I let my daddy down and my sister won't even talk to me. I haven't seen my kids in so long that I'm sure they forgot all about me." I bit my bottom lip the way I always did when I was embarrassed. I wasn't in the habit of telling my personal business to strangers, but it felt good to talk to someone about what was on my heart. Most people ignored me, but this man was different and I was happy that he seemed to care.

The man frowned. "You have very sad life. Back in Lebanon, family is everything. But here in America, it seems like people don't care about family."

"My family used to care, but things are different now."

"I hope things will be like they were again." He extended his hand. "Do you want refill?"

"Yes, please." I handed him my cup.

After guzzling down my second Coke, I asked, "Do you know what time it is?"

He pulled his cell phone out of his pocket. "7:42."

"I've gotta be leaving now. Thank you, sir." I hurried to the door.

"You want something to-go?"

"Thanks, but I can't be late." I really appreciated his offer, but at that moment, I needed to make sure I was going to sleep in a warm, dry place. I had to get to the shelter before nine o'clock or else they wouldn't let me in.

I walked the six blocks to the bus stop. It was Saturday so I knew I was going to be waiting awhile. Overhead, the sky turned dark gray and I heard booming thunder. Seconds later, freezing rain fell. Like most of the bus stops in Detroit, this one didn't have a shelter.

I was soaked by the time the bus arrived. The driver glared at me as I swiped my bus fare card. I recognized him, he had seen my card get rejected before. I said a silent prayer that my card had enough money on it. I smiled when it was accepted.

I made my way to the back of the bus. My clothes were very wet, as if I had just taken them out of the washer. My feet felt squishy inside of my damp shoes and socks. I was desperate for a hot shower and dry clothes. I thought about going to Daddy's house, but I knew he didn't want to see me. My father was a goodhearted man, but some mistakes couldn't be forgiven.

I sat down and waved at the lady sitting across from me. "Excuse me, miss, do you know what time it is?"

She looked at her watch. "8:23."

As we neared the downtown neighborhood known as Cass Corridor, I asked the lady to check her watch again. "8:52."

I pressed the button for the bus to stop, but the driver kept driving.

"You missed my stop, sir!" I hollered.

"Calm down. I'm stopping." The driver pulled up to

the next stop.

I ran out off of the bus and turned the corner on Cass Avenue. I moved as fast in the rain as I could, jaywalking through traffic signs. By the time I made it to the shelter, I was out of breath and out of hope. The door was closed, indicating that I missed the cut off time. I knocked on the door anyway.

"We ain't takin' nobody else, it's after nine!" A man shouted from the other side of the door.

"Please, sir…"

"Sorry."

"Hey, Ree-Ree!" A voice called from across the street. Ree-Ree became my nickname when Nate first turned me on to drugs and I got caught up in "the life." Although I wanted to leave Ree-Ree behind, most of the times she was more present than my shadow.

I'm not getting caught up today, I thought as I turned in the other direction. The thunder boomed in the sky above. I could smell the oncoming rain.

"Ree-Ree!"

I finally turned around to see who it was.

Jackie

THREE

I slipped on my t-shirt and looked at myself in the full-length mirror. My fitted jeans showed off my trim waist and accented my curvy hips. My flat sandals beautifully displayed my pedicured toes. I unloosened my shoulder-length curls from the ponytail holder thinking about how much Patrick loved it when I wore my hair down. I rubbed a bit of moisturizer on my face. My sepia complexion was smooth except for a bruise on my jawline that was never going to heal. I put on a bit of lip gloss and smacked my lips.

As I looked around the bedroom I used to share with Patrick, I tried not to think about how much I missed him. I didn't want it to show on my face when he came for the last of his belongings. Today was supposed to be the official end of our three-year relationship, but I had other plans.

I heard the doorbell ring. I popped a peppermint in my mouth and rushed to answer it.

"Hey!" I opened the door.

Patrick walked inside. He was 6'2 with skin the color of cherry wood. His baldhead was clean-shaven. His dark gray mustache and goatee were neatly groomed. His fit body was clad in a Burberry green business suit. Although he was fifty-eight years old, he appeared far younger. Patrick was Hollywood handsome, and just like Denzel Washington, his looks only improved with age.

As fine as he was, I was still angry at his betrayal. But I willed myself to smile. *There'll be plenty of time for me to give him a piece of my mind* after *we get back together and I make it clear that he can never, ever do that again,* I thought. Diane was right. I didn't deserve to be cheated on, but one indiscretion (maybe more than one) wasn't going to make me give up on our relationship completely.

I inhaled his scent. "That's nice. Is that the Gucci cologne I got you for Christmas?"

"Where's my box?"

"Oh, just a sec, I'll get it for you." I walked into the kitchen feeling disappointed. I probably should have been more direct and answered the door in my lingerie. Surely, that would have inspired our reconciliation. But all wasn't lost.

I turned on the stereo and put in my Marvin Gaye's Greatest Hits CD. I skipped past "Let's Get It On" and played "Distant Lover." I thought it was a subtle but sensual song that echoed how I felt about him. I reached into the cabinet and took out two wine glasses.

"Jackie?"

"Yeah?"

"What are you doing?" He stood in the kitchen doorway.

"I, um...do you want red or white?"

"Neither! I came here for my box and that's all I came here for. You know what, forget it..." He walked toward the front door.

"Patrick!" I followed behind him.

He turned around. "I don't even need those old law books anyway. I've got a library full of 'em down at the office. I guess I was just holding on to them for sentimental reasons, they helped get me through law school..." He paused. "I shouldn't have bothered you. I know this is awkward."

"It doesn't feel awkward to me. I think fate brought us together today, just like three years ago. Can we please talk for a minute?"

He frowned and looked at his watch. "I don't have time."

"You've got a client meeting? Oh, I'm sorry, I don't want you to be late. Why don't we get together later on–"

"Actually, I'm done with work for the day, but I'm taking Ebony and the kids to Twelve Oaks."

I laughed to hold in my tears. It was hilarious to imagine Patrick, his twenty-nine-year-old girlfriend and her toddler twin boys walking around the mall. Passers-by would certainly assume that he was the *grandfather.*

But the most pathetic thing of all was that I was still in love with "Gramps."

"Are you finished now?"

I took a deep breath to stop myself from giggling.

"You're gonna have to accept that I've moved on. I wish you all the best, Jackie. I really do. But Ebony is the woman I want to be with."

"I'm going to make a prediction… In about a month, one of two things is going to happen. You're going to exhaust of playing daddy to her little brats and or you're going to get bored with her. What do you have in common with her anyway? When was the last time she went to the Wright Museum or to a jazz concert?"

"You're selling her short. But then again, you've always been judgmental. For starters, Ebony has class and I love her kids like they are my own. They keep me young."

"So you've found your fountain of youth and now I'm just supposed to accept what happened? You went behind my back and dated your little paralegal for six months and then you discarded me like trash."

"If you knew about her, why did you stay with me?"

"Because I thought it was a fling. I figured that when you got her out of your system, you would come to your senses. I never dreamed you would actually leave me for her. We had something special. Something real. You owe me better than that."

"What makes you think I owe you anything? You

aren't my wife."

"But—"

"You wanted us to be like a Oprah and Stedman. But, baby, I'm too old for a girlfriend. I want a real commitment."

"If you wanted to get married, why didn't you just say so?"

"What would have been the point? When we first met, you made it clear where you stood on that issue."

"So you're going to marry Ebony?"

"I think I'd better go. You're already upset enough as it is."

"Please don't tell me that you're engaged!?" I looked up at him with tears in my eyes. "You're right...you shouldn't have come here."

"Goodbye, Jackie." He turned his back on me and walked out the door.

I sat on the couch, sobbing into my hands for several minutes. After I gathered my composure, I went into the kitchen and poured myself a glass of wine and filled it to the brim. I got my cell phone out of my pocket and scanned my contacts. As I approached Diane's name, I stopped at Daddy. I pressed the call button and waited.

After several rings, I heard Daddy's old school answering machine beep. The gospel song "We've Come This Far By Faith" played for a few seconds, then I heard his voice say, *"You have reached the Foster residence. Please leave a message at the sound of the tone and have a blessed day."* Beep.

"Daddy, it's me..." I took a long sip of wine. "Did you know that studies say that a daughter's relationship with her father will impact the relationships she has with men for the rest of her life? What do you think of that, Daddy? I'd love to hear your Christian perspective on that!"

"Jackie?"

I hiccupped. "Daddy?"

"Hold on, sweetheart, let me turn off of the machine." I heard a clicking noise. "I think that did it."

"I can't talk right now, I've gotta go."

"No, no, please don't hang up. It's good to hear your voice. I've been praying for you."

"Thank you, but I've gotta go." I took another swig of wine.

"Okay. I'm not gonna keep you long. But before I let you go...are you all right?"

"Yeah."

"And how's Patrick?"

"I thought...you didn't approve of my relationship with him, why do you care about how he's doing?"

"I'm just asking, sweetheart."

"If you must know, he's gone."

"Gone, as in–"

"We broke up."

"Well, I can't say that I'm sorry."

"I knew you'd feel that way."

"What do you expect me to say? You two started off on the wrong foot. The man was married when you first got together."

"He was separated, Daddy. Patrick and his wife had been living apart for over a year when we started dating. I'm no home wrecker."

"It might make you feel better to justify what you did, but it doesn't change the fact of the matter."

"I've gotta go."

"So what happened? Are you okay?"

"Yes, I'm fine. And so is Patrick and his twenty-nine-year-old girlfriend."

"I see."

"That's all you have to say about it?"

"Patrick is a leopard who showed his spots long ago."

"I loved him, Daddy."

"You know you make me proud. I love showing off all those pretty pictures of yours and you've accomplished so much in your profession. But you've still got a growing to do when it comes to relationships. You're out here in the world like some lost teenager. I always pray that you will share your love with the right man someday."

"A man like you?" I took a long sip of wine.

"Jackie, why don't you come to church this Sunday?"

"No thanks, Daddy."

"All right then, you know I'm gonna keep asking until you do." He paused. "Have you heard from your sister?"

"No," I lied. If I told him the truth about hanging

up on her recent phone call, I knew he would have been disappointed in me.

"Well, I've been looking for her. I went to her house and her neighbor told me that she left there two weeks ago."

"It's sad to say, but we both know where she is."

"I hope and pray it's not true, but we've been down this road before."

"If you're looking for Rhonda you need to be real careful, Daddy. I hate to think about you in those dangerous places."

"I've got God to look after me. I know you're busy, sweetheart. I'm gonna let you go. I love you."

"I'll talk to you later, Daddy." I hung up the phone. I did love him too, but I hadn't told him that in many years. I finished the rest of my wine, reflecting on what he said.

In my heart, I knew he was right. Patrick wasn't the one. Diane said it too. But I didn't need either one of them to tell me. Patrick had showed his trifling nature from the beginning but I willed myself to look the other way because I didn't want to be alone.

Sometimes, I closed my eyes and pictured myself twenty years from now...a seventy-year-old woman surrounded by gray cats. Well, maybe not cats, I always liked dogs better. But given the choice between facing my golden years with a pet as my sole companion and having Patrick to fuss after, (even if he did stray from time-to-time) I'd much rather have Patrick. And he'd much rather have Ebony.

I swallowed the rest of my wine as tears filled my eyes. I had been through breakups before, but this one stung especially hard. I thought of my looming fiftieth birthday. Surely, there had to be more to look forward to in life. Daddy would say, *"Sweetheart, you need Jesus!"* But I felt like I needed the Father, the Son *and* the Holy Ghost.

I lifted my head up to heaven in prayer. "Lord, I know I don't talk to you as often as I should and I know I don't live according to Your word all the time, make that most of the time. I'm sure there are many more deserving people who could really use Your blessings right now... but I'm asking You to please help me get through this. Sometimes, I get so afraid, Lord. I feel like I'm living my life the wrong way for the wrong reasons. I know I need to make some changes and I'm gonna work on that with your help. Thank you for listening. Amen."

Rhonda

FOUR

A family used to live in this house. I could almost see the mama cooking in the kitchen making a stretch meal like casserole or spaghetti. I pictured some kids crowded on the living room couch, watching TV. Maybe *Facts of Life* or *Different Strokes*. Maybe it's the episode when Todd Bridges kisses Janet Jackson and the youngest boy points at the screen and says, "Ooohhh!" The other kids tell him to shut up. He runs into the kitchen to tattletale and the mama shouts for everybody to shut up or else!

But the house was empty now and the only family living here was a family of rats (the four-legged kind and the two-legged kind.) I sat across from the biggest one. He had corn-yellow buckteeth and ashy skin. The whites of his eyes were red, just like a rat's. I forgot his real name, so I just started calling him Ratman in my head. Maybe I called him that out loud too because I wasn't in my right mind.

Years ago, Nate and I used to party with Ratman

at an after hours spot downtown. I remembered him wearing sharp suits and driving a rotation of souped-up cars. Back then, he dyed his hair jet black and wore a jheri curl long after it went out of style. But now, his nappy, gray hair was matted like it hadn't been washed since the 80's. I wasn't sure how long I'd been in that house with Ratman. I had no sense of time.

Nate and I used to get high in the garage, in the early morning hours, while the kids and the neighbors were sleeping. I always showered after-wards and used plenty of mouthwash to get rid of the stench. I knew it was wrong, but I never stepped foot in a dirty place like this to get my fix. Now, I was too desperate to care.

I was surrounded by strange people and strange smells. All of them were just as ugly as the Ratman. Some of them shot up heroin, some of them smoked on crack pipes, some of them guzzled malt liquor out of forty-ounce bottles, some puffed cigarettes, some of them slept, some of them did nasty things to each other. I didn't watch it, but I heard them making noises like husbands and wives in bed. But I knew none of them were married, at least not to each other.

Ratman looked at my jacket on the floor. "What's this?" He pulled my picture out of the pocket.

"Don't touch that!"

He held my photo up to the window light. He stared at the image of me in my little black dress with my hair and makeup perfectly done. He licked his dry, crusty lips. "You used to be a dime, baby girl. Was that all your real hair?"

"Give it back!"

"I know you remember how I used to get down. I was one of the most famous pimps in this city! Max Julien in *The Mack* ain't have nothin' on me!" He stroked my photo. "A fine, young thing like you...girl, I would have turned your sweet stuff into a gold mine!"

"I said give it back!"

"What you actin' all uptight for? I took you in out of the rain and supplied you with everything you needed to feel good and now you got the nerve to dog me out."

"Can I just have it back? Please!"

He threw the picture at my feet. "I can't stand a broad who orders me around. You'd better chill out, Ree-Ree."

I picked it up and put it in pants pocket.

"Are you gonna apologize to me?"

I stared at him.

"If you fix that attitude of yours, I can hook you up with something real nice."

"Sorry," I uttered, thinking about how good it would feel to get high.

He laughed. "I like you. You ain't no different from all them other girls I turned out. Word around is that you a preacher's daughter. If only the good reverend could see you now!"

"Don't you say nothing about my daddy!"

"You in my house. I'll talk about whoever I want,

however I want!"

I stood up. "I'm leaving."

"Where you gonna go?"

"Back to COTS."

"You think they gonna let stay there, high as you is…"

I started toward the door. I felt dizzy and disoriented in my crack haze. I doubted I could find my way back to the shelter and even if I did, I knew Ratman was right. They weren't going to let me in. I stopped by the doorway and sat on the first stair. I broke down, sobbing like a baby.

"Don't be like that, girl." Ratman sat next to me and rubbed my back.

His touch made me uncomfortable, but I was too out of it to push him away.

"It's like I always say…life is hard till you wake up and stop tryin' to fight your true nature. Me and you, we junkies. We ain't meant to be out there in the world, waking up to no alarm clock and driving through rush hour to go to work and mowing the lawn on the weekends. Naw! That ain't no life for me and you. I know it and deep down inside, you know it too. If you keep tryin' to fight it, you only gonna make yourself crazy."

"I know I can be better than this. I want my kids back."

"Was you thinkin' 'bout them kids the first time you lit up that pipe?"

"Nate is the one who–"

"Put a gun to your head and told you to smoke crack?"

"It's not like how you're making it sound."

"We tell ourselves all types of lies to keep from owning up to reality. I'll tell you what, I lied to you."

"About what?"

"About that stash. You want some?"

I hesitated.

He smiled. "Girl, I ain't your daddy and I ain't gonna judge you."

When he mentioned my father's name, I prayed for strength and God gave me my answer. "No, I'm gonna try to sleep this off and go to back to COTS tomorrow."

He stood up. "I guess that leaves more for me." He took a few steps and turned around. Ratman smiled at me, exposing his buckteeth. "If you change your mind, I'm right here, baby girl. And let me tell you, this stuff I got is the truth."

"Naw, you go ahead."

***

Later that night, Ratman told me that he was going out to get something to eat. He asked me if I wanted to go with him. Even though I was hungry, I told him no. I didn't trust him. He promised to bring me back some food from a restaurant dumpster and left.

I balled up my jacket into a makeshift pillow. Even though I was in a corner several feet away from the human rats, their different noises made it difficult to relax. I heard screaming, grunting and one of them was howling. Outside the window, I saw a big, pale full moon in the sky. Daddy always warned me that the devil is always busy, but he puts in overtime whenever there's a full moon.

If it was a little bit warmer, I would have spent the night under a freeway overpass or a park bench at Belle Isle. But it was freezing in the house and I didn't even want to imagine the temperature outside. My teeth chattered as I lay on the floor. I closed my eyes. Despite the cold and the rat sounds, I was so tired that it didn't take me long to fall asleep.

I dreamt that Nate and I were in our king-sized bed and he was holding me in the spoon position. He kissed my cheek and whispered, "I love you." I smiled at him and turned around.

Instinctively, I opened my eyes and saw Ratman groping me. The dream had turned into a very real nightmare, as I feared for my life.

"Stop!" I tried to break away from him.

He gripped me tighter. "Relax, baby girl. What did I tell you about trying to fight your nature..."

"Get off of me!"

"I'm sick of you teasing me."

"Please, don't! Please!" I looked around the room. "Somebody help me! Please!"

"Ain't nobody here gonna save you, 'cause you and

I both know you don't wanna be saved." He climbed on top of me and pinned me down.

I clawed at his face, scratching as hard as I could.

He choked me. "I'm gonna teach you how to treat a real man."

I could barely breathe. "Please...please...let me go..."

"Not till I get what I want. You ready to stop fighting?"

I nodded.

He loosened his grip around my neck. I was too weak to fight Ratman, so I called on someone strong enough to defeat any devil. "God, please help me," I prayed aloud. "God, please get me out of this situation. If you help me, I promise I will never get high again. I mean this time! If you help me, I promise to turn my life around. Please, God! Please help me!"

"Shut up, the man upstairs don't want no parts of you."

I felt God's presence in that room and I knew what I had to do. I smiled at Ratman. "You're right. I ain't been nice to you at all. Let me make it right, baby."

"That's what I'm talkin' 'bout, baby girl." He started to take off his pants.

"Why don't you lay down so I can make you feel good..."

Ratman grinned. "Ooohhh weee!!! It's my lucky night! Ain't nothin' like a preacher's daughter." He anxiously climbed off of me and lay on the floor.

I kneed Ratman in his groin as hard as I could.

"One for me!" I kneed him again. "And one for the man upstairs! He's always listening!"

He let out a high pitch scream and covered his manhood.

I ran for the door. With every step, I felt joy in my heart. I was so grateful that the Lord spared me from Ratman's attack. I had no doubt that I was going to keep my promise to Him and leave that life behind.

Jackie

FIVE

One of the things I loved about my job was the natural light. The loft style photography studio was surrounded by large floor-to-ceiling windows. There were no partitions; all of the office spaces were open for collaboration. The walls showcased large prints of gorgeous photos, including four pieces of mine.

I shuttered at the memory of my first job after college doing data entry in a cubicle the size of port-a-potty. Those fluorescent lights zapped my creativity. It took three cups of coffee a day to cope with the monotony of it all.

Then, one morning, my alarm clock went off and I decided I was never going back there. I told myself I was stepping out on faith. I packed my photography portfolio and a suitcase and bought a one-way train ticket to New York City. I went to every publishing company on Sixth Avenue, demanding to show off my pictures. Looking back, I can't believe I had the nerve to walk into those offices without an appointment or a clue. But the associate editor at *Soul Beat* gave me the opportunity of a lifetime. I often wished I had that same courage when it came to my love life.

I sat at my desk and turned the picture of Patrick facedown.

"What's that all about?" Liz, the senior graphic designer glanced over at me. She had spiky black hair with purple highlights. Both sides of her nose were pierced along with her left eyebrow. She had a passion for painting abstract acrylics. Last year, I attended her big art show. I was appalled to see canvas after canvas of little colorful dots that resembled my nephew's preschool creations. Liz's work certainly wasn't my taste, but since she was such a sweet person, I just sipped my wine and told her that she had a "unique and bold flare."

"Talk to me, Jackie," Liz insisted as she pointed to the facedown photo of the man I loved enough to forgive most any indiscretion.

"Oh, um, we broke up over the weekend," I explained.

"Officially?"

"Yep."

"He was too old for you anyway."

"But apparently not too old for Ebony," I mumbled.

"Huh?"

"Nothing." I turned back to my laptop. Images of delicious ice cream sundaes filled my screen. "I need to look over these proofs before I email them to the client."

"Those are for the Sanders print ad?"

I nodded.

"I love my job. I can't believe we get paid to look at desserts all day. The only thing better would be if we got paid to eat them."

I laughed. "You know I try to avoid that stuff."

"That's probably why you can still fit into your prom dress. Look at me, I'm half your age and I already look like a before model for Weight Watchers."

"You're not fat."

"Yeah, but I could stand to lose a few." She stroked her neck. "I'm starting to get a double-chin and that's so not-cute. It's all Eddie's fault. Turns out that getting married is worse than the freshman fifteen."

"Well, I wouldn't have a clue about that."

"I shouldn't be talking about newlywed life after you just broke up. I'm sorry, Jackie."

"Don't apologize. I'm fine."

"What happened?"

"We just...grew apart."

"That's a bummer. Weren't you guys together for like two years?"

"Three."

"Wow, I didn't realize it had been that long. I heard it takes one week for every month you were together to get over a breakup so, let's see, twelve weeks times three comes out to thirty-six weeks. What's that? Six months."

"I hope it won't take nearly that long."

"Well, there is something that could expedite the process."

"What?"

"Never underestimate the power of the rebound."

"Definitely not. What I need right now is a hiatus to get in touch with my emotions. I don't want to complicate things with anybody else." I enlarged my best picture on the screen. "What do you think?"

Liz looked at my laptop and then she looked at me. "I think you need a..." She sang, "*R-E-B-O-U-N-D.*"

"You're crazy." I chuckled.

"Granted, I realize I'm no Aretha, but the point is that you need the distraction of a fine man to help you get past this." She pointed. "I bet one night with him would make you forget all about Patrick."

I looked across the room at a young, handsome man wearing a leather jacket, t-shirt and jeans. I took in his toned body and his bronze, sun kissed complexion. He had a short, wavy hair and a clean-shaven face. I felt instantly attracted to him.

"I bet he's one of the models for the underwear shoot," I said. "I thought that wasn't until after lunch. He's very early."

"No, he's not a model."

"How do you know?"

"Because he's our newest co-worker."

"You're kidding."

"No, he's a videographer."

"Did they fire Bob?"

"Bob is in Chicago on special assignment, remember? Or has our new video guy got you all out of sorts."

"Please, Liz. It's not even like that."

I felt my heart beat faster as he approached us.

"What's he coming over here for?" I panicked.

"Maybe to say hello. People do say hello to each other, you know."

I rushed in the other direction to the bathroom. Inside, I checked my reflection in the mirror. I fluffed my hair and pressed my lips together to help rejuvenate my reddish brown lipstick shade. I smiled big to make sure I didn't have anything caught between my teeth. After I was satisfied with my appearance, I walked out with my head held high. Maybe Liz was right; a rebound might be just what the doctor ordered.

The videographer was standing by my desk, talking to Liz. He had his jacket off and I couldn't help but notice his muscular chest and fantasize about touching it.

I walked over to them. Up close, he looked to be about thirty-five. I grinned at him, hopeful that he wouldn't mind dating an older woman.

He smiled back revealing his neat, porcelain-white teeth. "Nice to meet you, I'm Harold Brown." He extended his hand to me.

I shook his hand and kept holding on. I didn't want to let him go.

Liz cleared her throat.

"Oh, I'm Jacqueline Foster, but please call me Jackie. Welcome to our team. There's usually more of us here, but everyone else is out on shoots or filming on location today."

"Well, I'm grateful to apart of the team. I really look forward to working with all of you."

"And I look forward to working on you...I mean, with you too."

"Can you please let go of my hand now?"

I released his hand. "Oh, sorry about that. I'm so embarrassed."

"She's a little out of it," Liz offered. "Jackie just went through a rough break up."

I glared at Liz. She had no business telling him about my personal life.

He frowned sympathetically. "I know firsthand how difficult that can be. I'm sorry to hear about that."

"Please don't feel sorry for me. I've always felt that everything happens for a reason, even if the reason isn't obvious at first."

"Spoken like a very wise woman."

"Well, I don't claim to have all the answers." I bit my lip. I didn't want to be a "wise woman," that was one adjective away from being an "old woman."

"Would it be too much trouble for one of you ladies to show me to the kitchen?"

"I'm sorta busy right now, but I'm sure Jackie won't mind." Liz winked at me as she turned toward her computer screen.

"No problem, follow me," I said.

"The set-up here is real nice."

"Yeah, I always loved the natural light here."

He grinned. "Natural light really brings out the beauty in things."

Is he actually flirting with me? I thought to myself as I opened the door to the kitchenette. "The fridge is sorta small, so we try our best to not leave anything in there past a week. The coffee maker isn't brand new, but it gets the job done. And all the plates and utensils are in the cabinets."

"Thanks."

"Let me know if you need anything else."

He looked at me for a moment and I felt tempted to lean in for a kiss. He said, "I was wondering..."

"Yes?"

"Where are the coffee mugs?"

"In that cabinet up there. Help yourself to the coffee, Liz just made it an hour ago. It's still fresh."

"Thanks, but actually, I'm gonna make myself some of this." He took a bag of organic green tea out of his pocket.

"Oh, I love that brand."

"We can share it if you want."

"No thanks, I'm already caffeinated enough." I paused. "So, you go organic?"

"I'm not a fanatic about it, but I try to make healthy

choices." He opened the cabinet and grabbed a coffee mug from the top shelf. As he stretched, I watched his biceps and triceps in motion. "How about you?"

"Huh? Oh...I try to make healthy choices too."

He filled his cup with hot water from the coffee maker and steeped his tea bag inside. "So, I hear you used to work for *Soul Beat*. What was that like?"

"I loved it. I loved meeting celebrities and living in New York. I even loved the stress of deadline day."

"Sounds exciting."

"It was."

"Why did you leave?"

"Long story. The abbreviated version is that I got laid off and I ended up having to come home. But if I had the chance to go back to New York, I wouldn't hesitate."

He drank his tea. "But you're from here right?"

"Yeah."

"So is your family still here?"

"They are, but that's a long story and even the abbreviated version would take all day to explain."

"Well, maybe you'll tell me one day."

"Are you always this noisy? I feel like you already know too much about my personal life. Liz told you about my breakup and now this."

"We're going to be working closely together, I don't see the harm."

"So what about your personal life?"

"What do you wanna know?"

"Are you married?"

"Divorced."

"Is that a code word for separated?"

"No, I've been divorced for eight years."

"Kids?"

"I have a son. He's graduating from high school this year."

"You look kinda young to have a kid that old, were you twelve when you had him?"

He smiled. "Look who's noisy now. If you must know, I was twenty-five when he was born. Some people may still consider that young, but I think we can both agree that there's a big difference between twenty-five and twelve."

"So that would make you..."

"Forty-three."

Liz walked into the kitchen, holding a menu from Sala Thai. "Well, it seems you two are hitting it off. I think it's great when co-workers get along. I was just about to order. Did you guys want anything?"

"Yeah, could you please order me the Pad Cashew and a ginger salad," I said. *And I'll have the Harold Special for dessert,* I thought to myself.

Rhonda

SIX

I rang the doorbell. In the early morning hour, Kenmoore Street was quiet and dark. As a child, I was so scared because our house was walking distance from City Airport *and* Mount Olive Cemetery. Whenever I heard an airplane buzzing overhead, I prayed it didn't crash through our roof. And every time Michael Jackson's "Thriller" video came on TV, I screamed louder than the actress who played his girlfriend. I was convinced dead people were going to burst out of their tombstones and head straight for our doorstep. But Daddy told me, "Don't waste your fear on the dead, keep an eye on the living instead."

When Daddy bought the house forty years ago, he got a good deal on it. It was a few years after the riots and most of the white folks had left, or were trying to leave. Mrs. Budziszewski (the neighborhood kids called her "Mrs. B") was the only one who stayed put. She used to bake paczkis for the whole block every Fat Tuesday.

She often told me that I was pretty enough to be a movie star.

I glanced down the street at Mrs. B's bungalow. It was one of the few occupied homes on the block. There were a lot of vacant lots, abandoned houses and a few burnouts. The airport had closed years ago. There wasn't much left of the old neighborhood.

Standing on the porch made memories flash in my mind. I pictured myself at the age of seven, sobbing while Jackie poured peroxide on my bloody elbow. Sam, the boy who lived across the street had called me ugly and pushed me off of my bike. Jackie teased that he had a crush on me. It was my first lesson in the connection between pain and love.

I thought about the time when I posed for under the aluminum awning in my sequin prom dress. Jackie spent three hours on my hair and makeup. She even let me borrow her real diamond earrings. I never felt so pretty in my whole life. Sam was my date. By then, he was eighteen years old and so handsome that I had long forgiven him for pushing me off my bike a decade earlier.

Even though Sam drove his own car, Daddy insisted on chaperoning us for the entire night. He stood near the punchbowl, watching me and Sam dance under the disco ball. I knew he wouldn't approve of us grinding our hips with baby-making gyrations like my classmates. So I made sure Sam and I kept plenty of space between us as we moved to the music.

For dinner, instead of going to a nice, sit down restaurant like the rest of my friends, Daddy took us to the buffet at Ponderosa and gave a long-winded prayer about inner strength and denying temptation. Little did he know, Sam and I had been fornicating for over a year on the old couch in his mother's basement. But just like the scar on my elbow he caused years ago, Sam ended up leaving me with more bruises.

I rang the bell again. The rising sun painted the dark sky shades of purple and red. Dawn always made me feel the promise in every new day. No matter what happened the night before, there was always a chance to start again.

As I waited on the porch, I feared that I had wasted my last chance. I knew my father wasn't asleep. Daddy had been an early riser since his childhood days on a cotton farm, waking up to a crowing rooster named after the first black boxing champion. Even though he had left Jack Johnson and Friars Point, Mississippi behind over fifty years ago, Daddy still never slept in past six.

I knocked until my knuckles were sore. I wondered if my father was on the other side of the peephole, staring at me. Maybe he had decided it was too risky to let me back into his home and back into his heart.

"Daddy!" I kept on knocking.

I heard the door unlock. Then, the door slowly creaked open. My father's small dark eyes widened from behind his wireframe glasses. He raised his eyebrows, causing the wrinkles on his dark brown forehead to deepen. Daddy shook his head as he rubbed his gray beard.

He was wearing his flannel robe; sweat pants and the old loafers he always wore around the house. Daddy never went without shoes. He'd spent most of his childhood barefoot and he told us stories about stepping on nails, splinters and garden snakes. He spoke of one little girl in his town who died of lockjaw. So as long as Daddy was able, he planned on keeping his feet covered up.

"Lord help you," he uttered.

"Daddy…" I knew I smelled horrible and looked even worse, but the way Daddy looked at me heightened my shame. I kept my head down. I didn't want to look in his eyes and see his disappointed expression. *Coming here was a bad idea, I should have gone back to COTS,* I thought.

"Come in, we'd better get you out the cold." He wrapped his arms around me. His hug was strong, just like his love for me. I wiped away a tear as I pulled away from Daddy. If I was him, *I* wouldn't even touch me. I was so humbled by my father's love.

"I've been looking for you. Where have you been?"

"I…I know I said I would never…I didn't mean to… it gets real hard. I know you don't understand it. I don't even understand it myself."

I walked inside, grateful to feel the heat on my skin. Daddy always kept the furnace on high. Everything was familiar. Jesus on a wooden cross. The faint smell of collard greens from the night before (Daddy was an amazing cook.) Family pictures on the mantel going back three generations. The worn but clean brown carpet under my feet.

"I was just about to put on a pot of coffee, you want some?"

"Yes, please." I followed him into the small kitchen. I sat down at the wooden table. Through the open curtains, I saw the orange sun rising in the sky.

Daddy sat down across from me and placed his hands firmly on top of mine. "I've been praying for you, Rhonda. Every time I heard the phone ring, all I could do was hope that it wasn't the morgue calling."

"I know my limits, Daddy. I never overdosed or even came close to—"

"I don't know exactly where I went wrong with you. Lord knows your mama and I tried to—"

"Daddy, it's not your fault that I'm this way. It's not because of anything that Mama did. Please don't think that."

"God has blessed me with the strength to understand so much, but this is beyond my understanding. Rhonda, you have two beautiful children and a family that loves you. I don't see how you could…" A tear slid down his cheek. He took off his glasses and wiped his eyes. He took a deep breath.

"I'm sorry I let you down, but it's like I told you, this has nothing to do with you."

He shook his head and walked over to the coffeemaker.

He opened the cabinet.

I stood up. "Daddy, never mind about the coffee."

He turned around.

"What I need right now...if it's all right with you...I need a shower and some clean clothes and something to eat. Then, I'm gonna head back to COTS."

"You don't have to stay at no shelter."

"I want to get well. I really do, but I can't burden you. I need to do this on my own. If I can't do it on my own then it won't count. At least not to me. How many times have I come to stay with you and then after a few weeks or a few months, I go back to–"

"I don't know how much longer the Lord will give me on this earth, but I don't want to go to my grave with any regrets. You're my baby girl and it's my responsibility to look after you. I'd be less than a man if I didn't do all I could to–"

"There's no fixing me, Daddy. I have to fix myself, don't you understand that?"

"I'm not letting you leave here."

"I'm only gonna hurt you again. We both know that. Why even go through the motions? If I was you I wouldn't have even opened the door for myself."

"Well thank God you're not me." He smiled as he placed two coffee mugs on the countertop. "A spoonful of sugar and a splash of cream, right?"

Jackie

SEVEN

I slipped into my black leather high heels with red bottoms. I usually wore flat shoes when I did a photo shoot, but today felt like a special occasion because I was working my first gig with Harold. He was all I could think about as I picked out my wardrobe...fitted khakis, a beige shell top and a black blazer. I took my time with my hair and makeup. Then, I sprayed myself with perfume.

I heard my apartment buzzer. I rushed over to it. I tried to sound seductive, "Yes, who is it?"

"Jackie, it's me," Harold said.

I looked at my watch, it was two-thirty. All of my primping threatened to make us late for our three o'clock start time. Center Stage Studios had a policy about making sure we were on-site at least fifteen minutes before each gig.

"I'll be down in a sec." I grabbed my camera bag and tripod.

On the elevator ride down to the lobby, my heart

pounded. I was nervous and excited to be alone with Harold in his car. Most of the times, I met my co-workers at the location, but when Harold offered to pick me up on the way there, I was thrilled to make an exception.

The April sun shone down on me as I walked outside. It was the warmest day of the year so far at sixty-nine degrees. With each step, I realized that I'd barely thought about Patrick since the day I met Harold.

He got out of his shiny, black Ford Fusion. He flashed a big smile. "Don't you look nice."

"Thanks."

He opened the passenger's side door for me.

"Thanks again."

He reached out his hands. "I'll take those."

"Wow, aren't you Mr. Chivalry." I gave him my camera bag and tripod.

"My father raised me to treat women with respect."

"It certainly shows."

He put my things in the trunk and got into the driver's seat. He started the ignition.

"Are you still close to him?"

"Yeah, me and my old man are like best friends. But I'm sure you can relate to that." He drove toward Jefferson Avenue.

"What are you talking about?"

"Isn't your father Reverend Abraham Foster?"

"Yeah, how did you know?"

"Everybody knows Reverend Foster! He's truly a

. man of God. When I met you, I thought that maybe you might be his daughter, so I went to the website for New Kingdom Baptist and he had you listed in his biography. From what I read, it's obvious that he's very proud of you and your sister."

"Who asked you to Google my family tree?"

"I didn't mean to upset you, it's just that–"

"Since you took it upon yourself to do a little research about the Fosters, let me fill in the rest of the blanks for you. My sister is a crack head and has been for years. And as for me, I barely speak to the person you refer to as a 'man of God'."

"I'm really sorry–"

"Do you mind if we don't talk right now."

"All right, is it okay if I...turn on some music?"

"Yeah, that would be fine." I needed a soulful tune to get my mind off of what just happened. In just a few minutes, I had gone from feeling like a lustful teenager to an angry black woman. *What business did he have digging up the details of my family life?* I thought as I glanced at his profile. The only thing that had stopped me from cursing him out was the fact that he was so handsome.

He turned on the radio and the car speakers blasted with the Fred Hammond's "Everything to Me."

Harold sang along: *"Brighten my path to guide my feet. Anoint my head and fill my cup. Oh Lord You're everything to me..."*

"Can you please turn the station?"

"Why?"

"I grew up in the church, I've heard enough gospel songs to last a lifetime. Would it kill you to turn on some jazz or some R&B, or are you one of those Christians that doesn't listen to 'secular music?'"

"You're too beautiful to be so bitter about life. If you'd like to share what's on your heart, I'd be happy to listen."

"So I'm bitter because I don't want to listen to..." I shook my hands like I was at a revival and mimicked my father's southern accent, *"The Lord's music!"*

I heard a loud popping noise. Then, Harold lost control of the car. He straddled two lanes, nearly hitting a motorcycle.

"Watch it!"

"I think we've got a flat tire." He turned on his hazard lights and safely steered to an empty metered parking space on Brush Street.

"That's just right on time, isn't it?"

"Stop being blasphemous!"

"Fine. I won't say another word except to point out that we're twelve minutes late and counting."

"So I guess that's my fault?"

"No. But I've never been late before and in this economy, jobs aren't exactly in abundance and–"

"Could you please pray with me?"

"Right now?"

Harold extended his hand to me. I was frustrated

about our earlier conversation, the flat tire and the fact that we were running late, but the look in his eyes was too sincere for me to deny him.

"I don't really know how much this will help, but if it will make you feel better..." I took his hand.

He bowed his head and closed his eyes. "Lord, I want to begin by thanking you. I thank you Lord because we could have been in a car accident, but you spared us from that. In the big scheme of life, a flat tire ain't no big deal, so I'm not complaining Lord. Although we don't always understand your ways or your reasons, but I pray that you help us through this. And Lord, I also pray you keep an eye on Jackie. Lord please help her to smile because she's so beautiful when she does. In the name of Jesus, we pray. Amen."

"Amen." I couldn't help but grin.

He smiled back at me. "See, the Lord is already making things better."

I pulled out my cell phone and dialed the client's number.

"Hello?" Sherri answered.

"It's Jackie. I'm so sorry...I'm with the videographer right now..."

"What's going on? Where are you guys?"

"I know we were supposed to be there at three, but unfortunately, we've got a flat tire."

"Please hurry!"

"We'll be there as soon as we can. I promise."

She sighed. "Okay. I expect to see you within the half hour. Is that understood?"

"Absolutely. Let me get off the phone so we can get over to you."

"Sounds like a plan."

"I'll see you soon, Sherri."

I hung up the phone. "What do you think if we leave the car here and call a cab?"

"That should be all right."

"You don't have a bunch of parking tickets do you?"

"Back in the day when I was a young jitterbug, I messed around and got the boot on my hooptie."

"Young jitterbug?" I giggled. I caught myself before telling him, *"That sounds like something Daddy would say."*

"I was getting some carryout from Bert's and I walked out with my catfish dinner just in time to see the man snap that ugly yellow thing on my front wheel. Since that day, I make it a point to pay my parking tickets immediately."

I laughed, amazed by all of the different emotions Harold brought out of me in less than an hour. Patrick hadn't managed to make me feel as much in three years. I looked at the glow of his brown eyes in the sunlight and wondered why I was so drawn to him.

***

The ballroom at the St. Regis Hotel was filled with the who's who of the Detroit arts community. Harold and I worked fast to set up our cameras.

Sherri approached us. She was a petite woman wearing a black pantsuit. Her silk blouse revealed her ample cleavage. Today she wore a blonde lace front weave à la Nene Leakes, but Sherri constantly changed her hairstyle. I had no doubt that the next time I saw her; she'd have bright red spiral curls inspired by Kandi Burruss.

"Hello, hello!" She grinned at Harold. "Who do we have here?"

He extended his hand. "Harold Brown, nice to meet you."

She battered her fake eyelashes and shook his hand. "The pleasure is all mine."

"How are we on schedule?" I asked.

"Well, lucky for you, the press conference doesn't really start until four-thirty. I just told everyone three o'clock. After all my years in PR, I've discovered that CP time is a chronic illness in our community." She looked at Harold. "Could you please excuse us for a moment?"

"No problem."

Sherri and I walked to the corner of the room near the refreshment table.

"What's wrong?"

"Your question is all wrong. You ought to be asking 'what's right' as Harold being Mr. Right."

"Excuse you."

"What's the story with Harold? This whole flat tire business. I'm not buying it. I can tell what really happened…you two pulled over in a moment of passion and–"

"No! It was actually a flat tire."

"So why are you blushing?"

"I'm not. Harold is my colleague. That's all."

"So it's safe to assume you don't mind if I make my move. What do you think of Mrs. Sherri Brown? I never wanted to be a Brown. It's such a plain last name and Lord knows there are already too many black people named Brown, but for a man of his quality, I could reconsider."

"He's not your type, Sherri."

"Why's that?"

"He's saved."

She blinked. "I'm offended that you think so little of me. You best believe I've saved my share of souls in the midnight hour."

"That's just wrong." I shook my head.

"I'm just speaking the truth, Sister Jackie! I have what it takes to deliver that Christian man over and over again."

"You really shouldn't talk like that. It's offensive."

"Don't tell me you've caught religion all the sudden?"

"I didn't say that, it's just that if you want a man like Harold…"

"Sherri!" A young man in a business suit waved. "Five minutes till start time."

"I'll talk to you later on, girl," she said as she walked

toward him.

***

Harold and I worked well together recording the press conference of college scholarships for Detroit Public School students who excelled in the arts. Sherri was happy that the event was a success and she thanked us as we broke down our camera equipment. She also slipped Harold her business card and winked.

"I'd love to work with you again, let's discuss it over dinner sometime," she said. Then, she sashayed out the door.

Harold put the card in his pocket.

"Are you going to call her?" I asked.

"Well, I–"

"Never mind. It's none of my business." I put my tripod back in its case and zipped it up.

"Sherri seems like a nice lady, but she isn't exactly what I'm looking for."

"Oh," I said feeling relieved. Sherri definitely had her share of suitors. Although she had an average face, her Coca Cola shaped figure made her a certifiable "brick house."

"I'm sorry if I offended you, I know she's your friend."

"I doubt she'll be bent out of shape if you don't call. She's got plenty of options. And I'm sure a man like you has his share of options too."

He smiled. "But quantity doesn't always equate to

quality."

"So if Sherri isn't what you're looking for, then what are you looking for?"

He kneeled to zip up his camera bag and looked up at me. "I'll know when I find her or maybe I should say when God sends her to me."

"That sounds pretty deep." I took a deep breath. "Harold?"

He stood up. We were face to face.

"I...um...I wanted to apologize for being blasphemous. It was wrong of me and I'm sorry. As you can probably tell, I don't have a very high opinion about my father and that has affected the way I feel about church in general. I was baptized as a baby, but I'm not what you would call a practicing Christian anymore. Despite that, I've always believed in God and I never want to disrespect Him. Even though I blamed you for the flat tire, I know it's my fault. Deep down inside, it was just God's way of reminding me of His power."

He put his hand on my shoulder. "Thank you for sharing that. And just so you know, I could tell from the moment I met you that you believed in the Lord. You have this aura about you that says you hold Him in your heart. But I'm sorry that you and your father aren't close anymore. I've heard him preach a few times before and I was always struck by his humility and devotion to the Lord. I couldn't imagine what happened that caused–"

"Trust me, it's a story that you don't want to hear."

"Sounds more like you're not ready to talk about it. I understand and respect that. But I'm here to listen whenever you want to share."

"Thank you."

"Are you hungry?"

"I'm starving! Sherri skimped big time on the refreshments."

"I say we get a cab back to my car and let's just hope the meter maid didn't leave too many tickets on my windshield. Then, we can grab a bite."

I smiled. "Sounds good."

Rhonda

EIGHT

The church basement was drafty. I could see bits of the sun shining through the glass block windows. It was actually warmer outside. But the cold I felt had more to do with my emotions than the temperature. As I sat in a circle of folded chairs, looking at the faces of people who had a terrible thing in common with me, I wanted to be somewhere else. Anywhere else.

A thin, balding man named Charles sat next to me. He said, "I asked my mother to loan me a hundred dollars. I told her that I wanted to buy my son something for his birthday. She asked me which one. As sad as it is for me to admit it, I've got nine kids by six different women. And worst of all, I ain't been a father to none of them. To tell you the truth, I don't know their birthdays. I barely even know their names. I was just using that as an excuse to get my hands on some of Mama's money.

"I was sure she was gonna give it to me, you know? Even if she thought I was lying, I figured she would take

72

the chance that I might do the right thing. Mama felt more guilty about me not being there for my kids than I did. I was too busy getting high off of alcohol, weed, crack and females. Whenever I laid down with a woman, it made me feel like a man, if only for a little while. I might even have more than nine kids, to be honest.

"So like I was saying, I asked Mama for the money and she told me she didn't have it. But I knew she did because I was looking through the mail and I saw her tax refund check. I begged her for that money. I knew a hundred dollars wasn't no big deal. But Mama said, 'I'll feed you and I'll give you a place to lay your head, but I ain't giving you a dime.'

"When she said that, this anger come over me. It was like the devil himself possessed me. I felt my fist balling up and before I knew it, I raised my hand up in the air and I looked down at her. Mama had this look in her eyes that I'll never forget. She screamed out. I came to my senses right then and there."

Charles bowed his head and sobbed. "I couldn't believe I almost hit the woman who brought me in the world...the person who loved me more than I ever loved myself. I've heard a lot of y'all talking about hitting bottom. Let me tell you, at that moment, I was below the bottom. I knew I was done with getting high. I could never hurt Mama like that again. And by God's grace, I've been sober for three years, seven months and twelve days."

"Thank you for sharing that with us, Brother Charles," Reverend Watkins said. He was the assistant pastor at my father's church and a recovering addict himself. I had been to several of his Narcotics Anonymous meetings before through the ups and downs of my journey to sobriety.

Everybody looked at me. It was my turn. My heartbeat doubled.

"Sister Rhonda, do you wish to say something today?"

"All of y'all have heard my story before."

"Tell us again. It helps you stay strong," Charles said.

"I'm inclined to agree with Brother Charles," Reverend Watkins added.

I took a deep breath. "My name is Rhonda and I'm an addict."

Several people said, "Hi, Rhonda."

I kept my head down to avoid eye contact with them. "It's never easy to talk about these things. The more I talk about it, the worse I feel about it. I just wish there was a way I could erase most of my life. The only thing I've got to be proud about is my kids. And I pray everyday that I can make them proud of me too. I can't even imagine what they go through knowing that they got a crack head for a mama."

"I think about how it was before I got turned on to drugs and I'd do anything to go back to those days. I guess it all started when I got married the first time. I was practically a child bride. I turned eighteen two weeks before the wedding. We were both too young, but we did it because I was in the family way.

"It seems sorta cliché but I'm one of those girls who married the boy next door. Well, Sam actually lived down the street, but he might as well have been next door. We had been going steady since I was in middle school. His love was the only kind of love I knew.

"When Sam got hired at the plant, we saved up enough money to buy a little house of our own. We needed the space. Jaimaya was toddling around and I was pregnant with our second child. After work, Sam went out with the fellas to bowl and drink beers. He started coming home later and later and I was real upset about it. To tell you the truth, I was jealous. There I was, cooped up in the house and he was out having himself a ball.

"One night I stayed up, waiting for him. The second he walked through the door, I told him that he needed to stop spending so much time away from home. And you what he said? 'Where's my dinner at?' He said it like I was his maid, not his wife. So I called him a name that I'm not gonna repeat in the house of the Lord. Then, Sam slapped me across my face so hard that I fell on the floor.

"That night was just the beginning of the abuse. It got so bad that I wore sunglasses all the time to cover up my black eyes. Strangers used to ask me if I was blind. I ended up having a miscarriage. It killed me inside to lose my baby boy. Sometimes, I would be wide awake and I'd hear a newborn crying. I knew it was my son. I felt like I was going crazy.

"I went to the doctor and he gave me some pills to make me feel better. And they helped. I stopped hearing the crying baby. I felt normal again. But Sam was still beating on me. One day, I was feeling so bad that I took more pills than I should have. Jaimaya found me passed out on the living room floor. She was screaming, 'Mommy!', 'Mommy!' I think she was about five or six at the time.

"That was my wakeup call to leave Sam. After my divorce, I felt free. Jaimaya and I lived in a nice apartment in Southfield. I took her to school every morning, then I went to my job at Providence Hospital. I worked as an orderly. It wasn't the job of my dreams, but helping people made me feel good.

"I was focused on taking care of my daughter. I started taking some weekend classes at Wayne County Community College so I could become a nurse one day. I was too busy to even think about dating. But one day, on my lunch break at Lou's Deli, this good-looking man started flirting with me. He offered to pay for my corn beef sandwich. To make a long story short, he gave me his business card. His name was Nate. Turns out, he had his own construction business. Nate kept trying to get me to go out with him. And after a few weeks, I gave in, but it wasn't the hot date he had in mind. I made him meet me here for the eleven o'clock service."

A few people laughed.

"Yeah, he thought it was funny too, but when he showed up that Sunday morning wearing his business suit, I have to admit that I was impressed. So was Daddy. Nate was the only man my father ever liked. We started spending more and more time together and he got along real good with Jaimaya. A year later, we got married. A year after that, my son Antoine was born.

"Nate insisted that I quit my job to stay at home and take care of the baby. And what a home it was! We had a seven-bedroom mansion in Bingham Farms. For my birthday, Nate bought me a brand new Range Rover. Life had never been so good.

"But everything changed the night I caught him in the master bathroom snorting cocaine. I couldn't believe he would do that. I was so hurt, but he said, 'You gotta believe me when I say I'm not hooked on this stuff. How could someone as successful as me be an addict? But if it bothers you that much, I promise not to ever bring it in the house again.'

"I wanted to believe him with everything in my heart. Nate was a good man and a very good provider. He had never raised his hand to me. He was the best husband I could ever hope for, so I trusted him and backed off.

"Then, one night, we went to his brother's birthday party at a club. By the end of the night, everybody was tipsy, including me. Nate reached into his pocket and pulled out a bag of white powder. He told his brother, 'I love you man, I got this for you. I can't think of a better way to celebrate.' Nate poured it on the table and his brother did a line. He screamed out like he was having the time of his life.

"Then, he asked if I wanted some. Nate put his arm around me and said, 'Naw man, my wifey is drug free.' Then, Nate did a line and grinned like he'd seen the gates of heaven open up. A few of his friends took turns. They all looked like they were having so much fun. I felt left out. Finally, I said, 'I think I'll try a little.' Nate asked, 'Are you sure, baby? Ain't no going back when you cross this line.' I laughed. 'It's not like I'm gonna get strung out after one hit.'

"But that's exactly what happened. When I was a teenager, I smoked weed once. All it did was make me cough and crave Doritos. But that cocaine was something else. And it didn't take long before I got turned on to crack. I lost all sense of reason. It got so bad that I sold my wedding ring, my engagement ring, the furniture, the TV. Nothing was off limits. I even sold my Range Rover.

"Nate put me out and filed for divorce. He ended up getting custody of the kids because he had adopted Jaimaya. I moved back in with my father for a while, but the streets kept calling me. I've been sober for as long as year, but I just can't seem to stay that way. I hit bottom two weeks ago when a man tried to rape me in a crack house. I haven't gotten high since that day and I hope that God will give me the strength to be done with drugs for good."

Jackie

NINE

I parked on Patton Street in front of Diane's house. I grabbed the grocery bag on my passenger's seat. The moment I closed the driver's door behind me, I pressed the car alarm button on my key fob three times. As I walked up to the front door, I said a silent prayer that my Chevy Impala would remain intact during my visit. Diane's block was in transition. Years ago, Brightmore had a reputation for its beautiful solid, brick homes and tree-lined streets.

Now, the neighborhood was known as "Blightmore" because of all the empty houses. Renters were beginning to outnumber homeowners. Crime was on the rise.

Diane and Tom's home had been broken into twice in the past five years. But they couldn't afford to move. They already had two mortgages on their small three-bedroom house.

I rang the doorbell. "Hey, girl, it's me!"

"Just a minute!" Diane called out from behind the

door. She was the busiest lady I knew, but I was so happy that she always made time for our friendship.

Diane opened the door and grinned at me. Her hair was freshly done in loose curls. Instead of the sweat suit she usually wore around the house, she had on jeans and a button-down shirt.

"You look good, girl." I hugged her.

"I'm only trying to keep up with you."

I smiled as I pulled a bottle of Chardonnay out of the grocery bag. "Look who got the last bottle of the good stuff! I'll put it in the freezer so it can chill."

Diane practically snatched the wine out of my hand. "I'll take care of it. Why don't you go in the living room and start up the DVD..."

"Are we really going to waste our girl's night in watching another Tyler Perry flick?"

"What do you have against Tyler?"

"He can start by ditching that gray wig and the moo moo."

"I don't know what's wrong with you, girl. Madea is hilarious, plus she tells it like it t-i-is!"

"Okay, if you say so..."

"Let me go and put this in the freezer and get the chips and salsa." She disappeared into the kitchen.

I walked into the living room and sat down on the couch. I glanced up at all of Diane's family photos on the mantel. I thought about how ironic it was for me to be a photographer with no pictures of my own relatives around my apartment (with the exception of Aunt Rose.) On my living room wall, there was a black and white image of her standing barefoot on the Mississippi farm where she grew up with my father. She had given me the photo at the lowest point in my life and I treasured it more than all of the pictures I had ever taken of celebrities and dignitaries.

"Did you start the movie yet?" Diane walked into the living room holding a tray of chips and salsa.

"Actually, I was hoping you might have a change of heart…" I unzipped my purse and pulled out the DVD of Denzel Washington's latest movie.

Diane frowned. "What's it called?"

"*2 Guns.*"

"It looks violent."

"Come on, girl. We need some action up in here."

"Let me think about it, but why don't we get that wine first…"

"You think it's chilled already?"

"You know how janky my freezer is. It won't make much difference if we wait another minute or another hour. I'm going to ask Tom to get me a new refrigerator for our anniversary. I want a stainless steel Whirlpool."

I chuckled. "You know you've been married too long when you start wanting appliances for your anniversary."

"Speaking of marriage, what's up with you and Harold?"

"We've gone out to dinner twice. That's all. There's

been no mention of putting a ring on it."

"But you like him?"

"He's growing on me."

"Whatever, girl, I know you. I can tell you're into him."

"I'm not really trying to mess up things at work by getting involved with a co-worker. Harold and I are just friends."

"Mmmhmmm."

"What's that supposed to mean?" I followed her into the kitchen.

"Surprise!" Several people shouted as I walked inside. A camera flashed bright in my eyes. I looked around the crowded room at Diane's husband Tom and their son, Byron. Liz from work and her husband, Craig stood near the doorway.

Sherri leaned on the kitchen counter. I didn't recognize her at first because she was wearing a bigger than life Diana Ross wig. But of all the people there, I was most shocked to see Daddy and Rhonda.

The last time I saw Rhonda, her hair was stringy and dirty. Today, it was cropped short and dyed dark brown. The style looked attractive on her. Her smile looked nearly perfect.

I assumed she was wearing dentures because Rhonda's drug use had ruined her real teeth. Although she was still skinny, she had picked up few pounds. From the looks of it, she had probably been clean for a month.

Maybe less. It was always hard to tell with Rhonda. She slipped in and out of her addiction so often.

Daddy stood next to Rhonda. He was wearing a gray suit and black wing-tipped shoes. At seventy-eight years old, my father was still a striking man. Most people just assumed he was in his late sixties. He attributed his youthful appearance to righteous living. Despite his lifetime of good deeds, Daddy and I knew that he hadn't answered for his greatest mistake.

I wanted to run for the front door, jump in my car and speed off. I didn't care one way or the other about what Daddy or Rhonda would have thought, but I knew that reaction would have hurt Diane's feelings. She had gone through all of this trouble to throw a surprise birthday party for me and the least I could do was suffer through it.

I looked down at the decorated cake that read: *"Happy 50th Birthday Jackie!"* Diane lit a big "5" and "0" candle. I was grateful that she hadn't placed fifty individual candles on the cake. I smiled to myself at the thought of those fire department jokes.

Diane started singing "Happy Birthday" and everyone joined in. When it was time to make a wish, I could only think of one thing. *Please let this party be over soon,* I thought as I took a deep breath and blew out the candles. Everyone clapped and cheered.

Diane handed me a cake cutter. "The birthday girl gets the first slice."

"Thanks." I cut myself a small piece. In my mind, I counted the calories of my sugary indulgence. It was going to have to spend an hour on the treadmill to burn it off. But I wasn't too concerned about my diet. All I could think about was Daddy and Rhonda. I intentionally turned my back on them.

"Would you like some ice cream?" Diane opened her freezer.

"No thanks, but how about that wine?"

"Of course."

"You got me good, girl. I would have never guessed what you were up to."

She smiled. "That look on your face was priceless."

"You'd better delete that photo or else," I teased.

Liz walked over to me, holding a shiny gift bag. "Craig and I can't stay, his mom is having a barbecue. But we picked you up a little something. I hope you like it."

"Thank you." I hugged her. "I'll see you on Monday."

"I really thought that Harold might be here."

"I'm kinda glad he isn't. I want him to keep thinking I'm in my forties." I winked.

"What are you so worried about? Fifty is the new thirty."

"That's easy for you to say at the age of twenty-five."

"I'll have you know that I'll be twenty-six in two weeks."

"Well, excuse me!" I chuckled. "I'll see you at the

studio, girl." I waved to Craig. "Thanks!"

"You're welcome," he said as they headed toward the door.

Diane poured me a glass of Chardonnay. "It's not exactly chilled, but I could throw in a ice cube if you want."

"No thanks." I didn't want to dilute the wine. I needed every drop of that alcohol at that moment.

Daddy and Rhonda walked toward me. I took a big gulp from my glass.

"Happy birthday, sweetheart." Daddy wrapped his arms around me.

"Thanks." I hugged him back slightly.

"Happy birthday, big sis!" Rhonda squeezed me.

"Thanks." I looked into her eyes. "How are you holding up?"

"I'm blessed."

"Your sister has been sober for twenty-six days, isn't that something?" Daddy added.

"It's been twenty-seven days if you count today, Daddy."

"Even better. It just goes to show how God is able." He paused. "We're not going to stay long, sweetheart. But I just wanted to let you know that the box with the blue and white wrapping is from us."

"You didn't have to get me a gift."

"What kind of father would I be if I didn't get something nice for my baby girl on her birthday?"

Don't get me started on the kind of father you are, I thought.

"Well, we'd better get going now. I've got a prayer meeting tonight." He kissed my forehead. "You take care of yourself, sweetheart."

Rhonda gave me another big hug. "I love you, big sis."

"I love you too."

After they left, I swallowed the rest of my wine. Sherri walked over to me.

"Happy birthday, girl! I would have never guessed you were fifty."

"Well, I do try." I fluffed my hair.

"So what's your secret?"

"Hitting the gym three times a week."

"And getting your cougar on...Diane told me that you and Harold are getting serious." She raised her painted eyebrows.

"We're only six and a half years apart, that hardly classifies me as a cougar. But we're not officially dating, so it doesn't matter anyway."

"Girl, please, that's your man. I knew something was up when he didn't call *moi!* Why didn't you just tell me you two were an item?"

"Because we're not."

"I get it, you're tryin' to be all hush-hush about your love life. For all I know you two might have had a secret wedding like Janet Jackson did. Was it two or three times that she snuck off to the altar?"

I laughed.

"No, but seriously, how do you feel?"

"I feel pretty good. I'm grateful to have my health and my career–"

"And your young tender."

"Girl, quit." I smiled and shook my head.

Diane poured a glass of wine for herself and Sherri. "I'd like to propose a toast... To the birthday girl..."

"I'll drink to that." The three of us clinked glasses.

Later that night, I unopened my gifts. Craig and Liz bought me the cute silver and turquoise bracelet that I'd been eyeing for weeks online. Diane and Tom got me a Kindle (I'd always wanted an e-reader, I couldn't thank them enough.)

Daddy got me a beautiful vase. Inside of my birthday card was a note written in his neat penmanship: *"You'll always be my baby girl, no matter who old you are. I love you so much and I will always be proud of you. I wish you would come around more often. I decided to get this for you in light of how you inherited your mother's love of flowers. Love Always, Daddy."*

Rhonda had sighed a separate birthday card. Inside, there was a fifty-dollar gift card for Macy's. Her note was even more basic: *"Happy Birthday Big Sis! Treat yourself to something special. Love, Rhonda."*

I was touched by Daddy's and Rhonda's gifts, but seeing them changed my mood. It should have been a festive occasion, but memories of the past made it impossible for me have a "happy" birthday.

Rhonda

TEN

I grinned at my reflection in the three-way mirror. Eleven weeks of staying sober and indulging in Daddy's down home cooking had transformed my body from a malnourished Size 0 to a curvy Size 4. I looked at my profile and chuckled at my little potbelly.

The store attendant asked, "Do you want to try the next size up?"

"Yes, please," I said. The sundress was snug on me.

"I'll go get it for you."

"Thanks." I walked back to the dressing room and took off the dress.

I stood in my underwear, staring at myself. My body was a roadmap of bruises, from my C-section scar to the marks from my many battles with Sam to the dark spots that appeared when I first got hooked on drugs. I remembered how pretty and smooth my skin used to be and I wanted to cry. It didn't matter if I never used drugs again, the evidence of my past was going to last a lifetime.

Someone knocked on my dressing room door. "Miss, are you in there?"

I swallowed my tears.

"Miss?" She knocked again.

"Yeah." My voice cracked.

"I found that dress in a Medium. Would you still like to try it on?"

"Okay." I cracked the door open and took it from the attendant, fast so she wouldn't notice me crying. I shut the door.

"Are you all right, miss?"

I took a deep breath. "I'm fine."

"Okay. Please let me know if you need anything."

I listened to the sound of her high heels walking across the tiled floor. When she was gone, I sank down to the floor and sobbed into my hands. As a child, crying was the only thing I could do to feel better. But now, each tear brought on more sadness. I envied people like my sister who could shut off her emotions like a faucet. It would be a blessing to be numb just like Jackie. She didn't seem to care about me or Daddy or much of anything besides her job.

But my heart was wide open. I even felt bad when I stepped on an ant by mistake. God made everything and every living being deserved a chance to be happy, at least that's what I thought. I hated to see suffering. Nate used to get upset with me because I gave away money left and right to folks in need.

I never judged people, no matter how down and out they were. One February, Nate and I were leaving a restaurant downtown and I saw a homeless woman standing by a traffic light. She had on a thin trench coat. There was a half a foot of snow on the ground. I asked him to pull over. I got out of the car and gave the woman my mink coat.

She thought it was a joke. It took a few minutes to convince her that I was serious. She was so grateful. She wrapped her arms around me and said that there was a spot for me up in heaven. I'm not sure if I've earned a spot in God's kingdom, but I wanted nothing more than to follow His path for me.

"How does it look?" the attendant asked.

I stood up as I wiped my eyes. "It's nice. I think I'm gonna buy this one and look for a necklace to go with it."

"Great, I'll be at the register when you're ready." She walked away.

After I calmed down from my crying fit, I tried on the dress. I looked at myself and saw pieces of the beautiful woman I used to be. *Maybe I can be that Rhonda again,* I thought.

I walked out of the dressing room, still wearing the dress. The attendant smiled at me from behind the register. "It looks pretty on you."

"Thanks." I kept my head down. There was a time when I would have believed her, but now I was so self-concious about my appearance that I questioned all compliments. Earlier that day, as I walked around Eastland Mall, whenever someone passing by made eye contact, I was sure that they were thinking "crack head." I doubted I could ever be free of that label.

"Are you going to get that necklace?"

"Maybe next time." I paused. "Is it okay if I wear this dress out of the store?"

"Sure. I can't blame you. That won't be a problem at all." She punched something into the register and said, "Your total is $52.98. Would you like to apply for a credit card today? You can save 10% on your purchase."

"No thanks," I said. I was sure that looking up my credit score would cause the machine to break. I was tens of thousands of dollars in debt, including child support (Nate had been awarded that too) and income taxes. But as soon as I was able, I planned to fix my finances, one payment at a time, even if I was Daddy's age by the time everything was paid off.

I opened my purse and pulled out my wallet. I handed her three twenty-dollar bills. It was the first time I'd bought something in a very long time. Daddy had given me two hundred dollars worth of shopping money. I loved him for trusting me. We both knew the horrible ways I could have spent that cash.

"Thanks and have a nice day." She handed me a receipt.

"You too."

The alarm sounded as I walked out. It brought back sad memories of when I stooped to shoplifting to support my habit. The security guard approached. "Don't move!"

"I just bought this, I've got the receipt right here." I opened my purse.

The attendant hurried over to me. "I'm so sorry, I should have taken care of this." She kneeled and used her machine to remove the anti-theft tag. "Once again, I am so sorry." She used a pair of scissors to cut off the price tag.

"Don't feel bad, it was an honest mistake," I said.

"Take care, miss."

"Thanks." I walked out.

The security guard snickered and said under his breath, "I thought I was gonna have to use my nightstick on that fiend."

"That's mean," the attendant said. But seconds later, I heard her laughing.

I hurried away from them so fast that I bumped into a man listening to his iPod. "Watch where the hell you're going!"

"Sorry, sir…"

He stepped back brushed himself off as if he was wiping away filth. Then, he turned in the opposite direction.

I cried openly as I reached in my purse and pulled out the pick-up-and-go cell phone that Daddy bought for me. I called his number.

"Hey, sweetheart, did you find a nice dress to wear for Sunday?"

"Daddy, can you...can you please come get me."

"What's the matter?"

"I just...nothing..."

"I'll be there in ten minutes. Wait for me in the spot where I picked you up."

"Okay."

"Are you gonna be all right?"

"Yeah."

"You sure?"

"Yeah."

"Okay, I'll see you in a few."

I hung up the phone and looked around at the senior citizens power walking, the mothers pushing their babies in strollers, the teenagers giggling and the employees ringing up sales. All of them looked normal and happy. I wasn't sure if I could ever fit into their world.

I thought about how low the store attendant and the security guard made me feel. I knew most people looked at me the same way they did. It seemed that nobody except my father saw me as a child of God. Everyday, I was going to have to battle that negativity just to be treated like a human being. I wondered if it was worth it.

I unzipped my purse and looked at the money. As bad as I felt, there was only one thing that could make me feel better. I had enough cash to get a cab to my old dealer's house and stay high for several days.

"Young lady?"

I turned around. An old woman wearing a sweat suit held up a receipt. She had broken away from the group of power-walking seniors.

"I think you dropped this."

I took the receipt. "Thank you, ma'am. You didn't have to go out your way for me like that."

"It's all in divine order because one day, I'm sure you'll go out of your way for someone else."

"That was very kind of you."

"Don't mention it." She looked at her friends walking up the stairs. "I'd better catch up with the rest of my golden girls. You have a blessed day, young lady."

"Thanks, you too."

As she walked away, I looked down at the receipt and saw that it was for a three hundred dollar men's watch. I smiled to myself at the realization that the woman had to be an angel God put in my path. I walked back to the main mall entrance to wait for Daddy.

***

"Hey, sweetheart." Daddy smiled at me as I got into the car.

"Hey."

"Now isn't that a pretty dress."

"It's been so long since I bought a new dress, I just couldn't let that lady at the store put it in the bag. I just had to wear it right away." I grinned.

"You seem to be in good spirits."

"I am," I said as I thought about the old woman who handed me the wrong receipt.

"When you called me earlier, I was worried about you." Daddy turned onto 8 Mile.

"Well, I'm okay. I'm just hungry."

"I'm surprised you didn't eat at the mall."

"What's the use in eating at the food court when my father can throw down in the kitchen like a master chef."

"Well, I appreciate the compliment, but I'm not cooking tonight. Sister Sadie is bringing over some of her meatloaf."

I smiled. "I wish you would have told me that. I would have picked up some Chinese food or something."

He chucked. "Oh now, her food isn't *that* bad."

"I know she's sweet on you, but have you forgotten how many Alka-Seltzers you needed after the last time she cooked?"

"Well, maybe we'll pick up a bucket of chicken."

"The Colonel sounds good."

"But you gotta cover for me and tell her that I forgot she was bringing dinner."

"I've got you, Daddy."

"It's too hot to be turning on the oven in this weather anyway. They say it might be 103 degrees tomorrow. So far, it's the hottest July on record. Of course this ain't nothin' compared to the heat back in Mississippi."

"Yeah, I remember all those summer trips down south, it felt like my skin was gonna melt off." I paused.

"Daddy, do you believe in angels?"

"Yeah. Why do you ask?"

"I think I met one today. When I called you to come pick me up, I was feeling so low that I…as soon as I got off the phone with you, I thought I might…but then, this old lady walked up to me and just seeing her smile reminded me that God is everywhere."

"That's such a blessing. I'm very proud of you, Rhonda. I know it's not easy to walk the path you're on."

"But Daddy, I'm gonna do whatever it takes to stay on it."

"I know you will."

"And I've been thinking a lot about Jaimaya and Antoine. I miss them so much and I want them back in my life. I feel like half of a woman without them."

"I miss them too. They're my only grandbabies."

"I don't know what it will take to get through to Jaimaya. I'm pretty sure she's written me off, but I'm never gonna stop trying. She'll always be my baby girl. And for me to see Antoine, I'm probably gonna need a lawyer, you know how Nate is."

"Never mind Nate. As a parent you still have rights. Let me talk to Deacon Lewis. His nephew is an attorney and if I'm not mistaken, I think he specializes in family law."

"I appreciate that, Daddy, but I know that lawyer's aren't free. I'm gonna look for a job."

"I'm real proud of you for taking that step, but are

you sure you're ready for that kind of responsibility?"

"It's time for me to handle my business like a grown woman. I can't keep spending my days feeling sorry for myself. Some of the happiest times I ever had was when I woke up everyday to get dressed for work. The check that came every two weeks wasn't just about money because Lord knows I never made a lot, but it gave me a sense of pride, you understand?"

"I do and you know I'll do whatever I can to support you."

"Naw, Daddy, it's important I do this on my own. I'm going to start filling out some applications."

He pulled up into the drive thru of Kentucky Fried Chicken. He grinned. "Today, I'm buying, but when you get that new job, it'll be your treat."

"Sounds good and I'll let you order the twelve-piece special with mash potatoes, gravy, corn on the cobb, biscuits *and* slaw!"

"Well, all right, if you put it that way, I can't wait for you to start working again."

We shared a laugh together. I felt a new purpose in my heart. I looked forward to turning on the computer after dinner and starting my job search. No matter the setbacks, I was determined to make the most of my life.

When I was a little girl, Mama used to tell me that God cared more about the inside than the outside. I knew a big reason why she spoke about inner beauty so much was because of the way her appearance had changed through the years.

I used to stare at my parents' wedding picture on the mantel right between my great-grandfather's Bible (that looked older than time itself) and a little wooden plaque that was carved with the letters: "LORD PLEASE BLESS MY LITTLE HOUSE."

On Mama's wedding day, she was a gorgeous nineteen-year-old girl with long, wavy curls (what the old folks called "good hair.") She was a little bit plump with round cheeks and generous bosoms, but her full figure was in proportion. Daddy was wearing a black suit and a matching hat. He was holding her tight; I'd never seen him look so happy.

But Mama looked completely different by the time I was born. Some of my earliest memories were of watching her get out of breath as she walked from the kitchen to the living room. Mama was nearly three hundred pounds and she suffered from diabetes and high blood pressure. Eventually, after her foot was amputated, Daddy pushed her around in a wheelchair.

Even though Mama wasn't pretty or healthy anymore, my father loved her just the same. Through all of my troubles, I came to know how deeply rooted his love was. It didn't matter what I'd been through, he always had room in his heart for me and I was humbled by this kind of love.

Daddy handed me the KFC bags. "I hope this won't hurt Sister Sadie's feelings too much."

"Huh?"

"Are you all right?"

"I was just thinking about Mama."

"We should pay her a visit and put some flowers on her grave after church."

"As long as they're tulips. Mama loved her some tulips, especially the yellow ones."

"Indeed she did... You know she would be real proud of you."

"And I don't want to let her down. You either, Daddy."

"You won't, sweetheart. Just keep walking with the Lord and you'll be fine."

Jackie

ELEVEN

The August sun beamed down as Harold pulled into the parking lot of Dexter Avenue Baptist Church. Men wore suits. Women wore dresses and matching hats. The heat had not deterred them from putting on their Sunday best. I was wearing my flowing flowered skirt and short-sleeved blouse. I hadn't bothered with any makeup at all with the exception of a little lipstick. My hair was pulled back in a bun.

"It's been a long time since I've been to church," I explained.

Harold pressed the button to unlock the doors. "No time like the present to turn that around."

I took a deep breath as I got out of the car. It was a shock to go from the comfort of air conditioning to the steamy humidity outside. Within a few seconds, I started sweating. But Harold looked so cool in his sharp blue suit and sunglasses.

"It's Africa hot today." I patted my forehead with

a tissue from my purse. I followed him as we walked toward the entrance.

"I'm used to this weather after all those years I spent in Atlanta. Sometimes, I think about moving back. How would you feel about living in the south?"

I shook my head. "Never again."

"Where'd you live?"

"I never technically lived there, but my father is from Mississippi. He used to drag us down there every summer to visit his kinfolk."

"Where?"

"Friars Point."

"So you've got a little farm girl in you, huh?"

"Definitely not."

He opened the door for me. I was grateful that the church's central air was working. My body felt cool within seconds. The usher smiled at Harold as we made our way into the chapel.

"Mrs. Coleman, I'd like to introduce you to my… um…to Jackie."

I shook her hand. "It's a pleasure to meet you."

"You too, honey." She winked at Harold.

As we made our way to a pew, I asked, "Why did you hesitate?"

"What do you mean?"

We sat down. "When you introduced me to her, you hesitated like you were going to introduce me as your–"

"Girlfriend?"

The blood rushed to my cheeks. Harold and I had been spending time together every week since the day we worked on Sherri's press conference together. We'd gone for long afternoon walks along the river and he had even talked me into trying the indoor mountain climbing wall at the YMCA. We had also enjoyed intimate dinners at restaurants and he even cooked lasagna at his house one night.

Although our intimacy had not gone beyond a kiss, the sensation of Harold's lips on mine made me feel alive with the kind of passion that my relationship with Patrick had lacked. Even though Patrick and I had explored every activity that a man and woman could try in the bedroom, Harold had touched me on a much deeper level. I never thought I would be head over heels for a celibate man, but I cared very deeply for Harold. I felt myself falling in love with him. Diane had the laugh of a lifetime when I explained the whole situation. She declared, "See girl, I told you so! When God puts the right man in your path, you'll do the right thing."

Harold touched my shoulder. "You never have to worry about me calling you my girlfriend because that's not what I want."

"Oh." My heart sank. For the past few months, I thought we were truly connecting, but maybe Harold just wanted me as a friend.

He kissed my cheek and whispered, "I'd much rather introduce you as my fiancé...and one day, my wife."

I grinned. "Is that so?"

"Faith without deeds is useless. Let me show you."

The choir started singing "What God Has For Me, It Is For Me."

Harold and I stood up along with the rest of the congregation. I used to have so many bad feelings about church, but I felt in my heart that today was going to be different. I put my family memories aside and clapped my hands. The music made my heart glad. I sang along. Growing up as a preacher's daughter, I knew the lyrics to all of the gospel hymns.

I looked at Harold's handsome profile as he hummed along. At that moment, I was in a place I never thought I'd be with the kind of man I never thought I'd ever be with in a city I never thought I'd come back to, but I was too happy for words. Daddy was right about one thing—*man plans and God laughs.* I thanked the Lord that I hadn't gotten in the way of His ultimate plans for me.

The church's pastor, Rev. Littlejohn, walked up to the podium. "How are God's people feeling today?"

"Blessed."

"Fine."

"Blessed and highly favored."

"Feelin' good, Reverend!"

"Well, Amen! I hope y'all don't mind if we deviate a little bit from today's service. Before I give the sermon today, I'd like to invite someone up here to talk to y'all. I'm honored to have a very special guest among us, a man I've looked up to since I was a little boy. There are some people who are put on this earth to preach God's word and he is most certainly one of those people.

"He called me up on the phone and said, 'We've got a problem in the community that needs fixing.' I offered to help out in any way I could. He's is just that sort of man. We all know people like that, don't we? When they call you up, there's just no saying no.

"The problem that we're talking about goes by many names. There's no need for me to sugarcoat it. I'm talking about heroin, crack, alcohol, prescription drugs; the list is far too long. And too many of our brothers and sisters have found themselves in the throes of addiction.

"These folks I'm talking about ain't *'them over there.'* They are our neighbors, our friends, our coworkers, our parents, our spouses; they might even be our children! And some of you might be thinking, it ain't me! It ain't none of my kin! It ain't my problem!

"But see, that's where you're wrong because it's just like I always tell you…there but for the grace of God go I! We should never stand in judgement. So when I got a call from our special guest asking to use our community center for outreach to help in the cause. I agreed right away.

"Some of you who have seen the man preach before might know him as Honest Abe, because just like the president who emancipated our people from slavery, he speaks the truth, even when it makes folks uncomfortable.

"Christianity isn't just about praising the Lord on Sunday morning and treating yourself to a soul food brunch afterward. Being a true Christian is about making yourself uncomfortable when God requires it. The man I'm about to invite to speak is a soldier in the fight against this devil that has claimed too many Christian souls. Without further ado, Reverend Foster of New Kingdom Baptist Church, come on up here…"

Everyone applauded as my father walked to the podium.

I turned to Harold. "You knew he was gonna be here, didn't you?"

"I…"

"How could you?"

He whispered, "Do you want to leave?"

What I wanted to do was stand up and tell the entire congregation the truth about "Honest Abe" but I was sure my testimony would give my father a heart attack. Despite all of my issues with Daddy, I didn't want to send him to an early grave.

"I'm sorry, Jackie."

"After he's finished, I want to get out of here."

"Okay." He held my hand.

Daddy surveyed the crowd and adjusted his glasses. I was glad that we were in the back of the church. I was sure that he couldn't see me and I wanted to keep it that way. I scooted over so that I was directly behind a woman wearing a massive hat.

Harold wrapped his arm around me. I felt a little stronger. *As soon as it's over, you can leave,* I reminded myself. I hoped that Daddy wouldn't be as long-winded as usual when he stood in the pulpit. He had preached his share of marathon sermons.

"Thank you so much for that warm welcome. It's an honor and privilege to be before you today. I want to begin by telling all of you that I've been preaching for longer than most of you have been alive. I was born in Mississippi, you see. My daddy was a sharecropper. Me and my brothers and sisters worked in the field picking cotton...*From can't see in the mornin' to cain't see at night,* as the old folks say.

"At night, my fingers were bloody and calloused. I'd ask my mama, 'If there's a God, and He loves me like you say He loves me then why does He make me suffer so?' And she'd tell me, 'Sometimes, the Lord will test you, just to make sure you're worthy.' At eight years old, let me tell you, that wasn't exactly what I wanted to hear, but the idea of God's test scared me. I didn't want to find out what would happen if I failed the test, so I devoted myself to Him. By the time I was thirteen, I'd read the whole Bible, cover-to-cover.

"And a few years later, God called me to become a preacher. I met my wife and we moved up here. We were blessed with a baby girl. From the moment she came into the world, Jackie was a spirited little child. She brought new happiness to our home.

"My wife and I wanted nothing more than for little Jackie to have a brother or sister. But after years of trying, my wife didn't get pregnant. We went to the doctor and he told us she was barren. He said she couldn't have anymore babies.

"Now, the good Lord tells us to be fruitful and multiply. My wife and I both came from big families and it just broke our hearts that we were going to raise an only child. Don't get me wrong, I was very grateful for Jackie. But it hurt us so bad that God denied us the joy of having a second baby. But it turned out He was testing us.

"A few years later, my wife got pregnant with our second daughter. It was such a surprise. Me and my wife were both in our mid-forties at the time! And we just loved that baby girl. Rhonda was our pride and joy.

"So there you have it, doctors don't know everything! God decides what happens and when it happens and how it happens. Me and my wife had never felt so blessed. But when our youngest was just five years old, the Lord called my wife home. I felt dead inside. God had given me another test…life as a single father was something I never imagined for myself.

"And I made some mistakes along the way, but I tried to raise my girls to love the Lord as I did. Both of them graduated from high school and seemed to be on the right track. Jackie finished college and became a successful photographer. Rhonda got married and started a family of her own.

"But a few years later, I faced another test and I call it my greatest test because it wasn't my test, although it felt like it was mine. My baby girl, Rhonda became addicted to drugs. As a result of it, she lost her home, her husband and her children. No amount of prayer seemed to make things better. She was living on the streets. Even though I told her that I wanted her to come back home, she wouldn't. She said she was embarrassed of what she had become.

"So here I am, a supposed man of God, with a child who…" Daddy took off his glasses and wiped his eyes. "With a child who was lost in the devil's world. I felt I had failed as a man and as a father. I contemplated my missteps over and over again. I spent my days thinking, 'What if I would have done this instead of that…'

"But you know what my biggest mistake was? I wanted things fixed on my schedule. I didn't respect God's timetable. You see, God had a plan for my daughter, but patience was the key. Could you stand up please, sweetheart?"

Rhonda rose to her feet. She looked better than she had in years. She had on a beautiful yellow and white dress that showed off her healthy figure. She wore foundation on her face to cover up her dark spots and blemishes. I started to cry. Seeing her renewed my spirit.

"My baby girl has been sober for five months. I am so proud of her. God tested our whole family, but He fixed everything on His timetable! Not yours! Not mine! But His! God's got His own appointment book and He don't care about yours! So I want to remind y'all that no matter what you're going through, He is able!"

"I'm just about done today, I wish I could stay and worship with you, but I've got to make the rounds to a few more churches. I feel that what I'm doing is apart of God's calling for me and I'm trying to get as many churches involved as possible. But before I leave, I wanted to let all of you know that Rev. Littlejohn has agreed to let us host a weekly Narcotics Anonymous at your community center here and for that, we are very grateful. Please invite folks in need to attend. There's no shame in it. And remember, everything can be made better on God's timetable. Thank you."

Daddy left the podium. I sobbed into Harold's shoulder as the congregation hollered out "Amens" and "Hallelujahs!"

Harold rubbed my back. Everyone applauded as Daddy and Rhonda walked down the side aisle. He shook a hands with a few church members. They walked out of the chapel. I was relieved that they were gone, but still overwhelmed by all of my emotions.

"Do you still want to leave?" Harold whispered.

"No, we don't have to." I paused. "I didn't mean to act that way...it's just so much between me and my father, you don't understand."

"Can we please talk about it after service?"

I took a deep breath. In the past, I'd only told my ex-boyfriends bits and pieces of the story. I'd never trusted any of them enough to share all of the details of what happened to me. But there was something in Harold's eyes that made me feel he was someone I could open my heart to.

Jackie

TWELVE
June 22, 1978

I leaned in close to my vanity mirror and put on some pink lipstick. My best friend, Diane gave it to me on the last day of school. She knows that Mama and Daddy don't allow me to wear makeup. The only thing I can to put on my lips is Vaseline.

But Diane's mother takes her to Hudson's to pick out sparkly eye shadows and perfumes that smell like sweet fruits mixed with the petals of pretty flowers. I'm jealous of Diane and her cool mother. Never in a zillion years would Mama take me shopping for anything besides plain-colored fabrics to sew into my ugly, shapeless dresses.

I blotted my lips with a tissue fifteen times until the bright pink color faded. Now, it was hard to tell that I was wearing lipstick at all, but I still knew it. And he would know it too. I smiled at the thought of him. In my mind, he was my husband already. At fifteen years old,

I knew I was too young to get married in real life. But I had no doubt that I was going to be his wife one day.

"Jackie!" Mama yelled.

"Yes, Mama, I'm coming..." I took one last look at myself in the mirror. I was wearing a pair of jeans my Aunt Rose had given me for Christmas and a t-shirt that was a size too big. All of my clothes were a little loose because Mama said it was important for me to not show off "my treasures." I tucked in my shirt, trying my best to show off my waistline.

"Jackie!"

I hurried into the living room. Mama was sitting on the couch, wearing a moo moo. She was so obese that she nearly took up two seat cushions. It was heartbreaking to see her. I had prayed many times for God to restore my mother's health, but through the years, she only gained more weight. I was determined never to let that happen to me. Even if I had to eat salads for breakfast, lunch and dinner for the rest of my life, I never wanted to be as helpless as Mama.

"I need you to go get my insulin."

"Yes, ma'am." I went into the kitchen and got her diabetes supplies out of the cabinet. I walked back into the living room.

I sat next to Mama and pricked her index finger with the small needle. Then, I put the droplet of blood on a strip of a paper to check her blood sugar level. A few seconds later, I prepared her insulin needle the way I had many times before. Mama rolled up her sleeve and closed her eyes. I inserted the insulin needle into her arm. She jumped slightly and took several deep breaths.

When I finished, she said, "I appreciate the way you look after me. I don't know what in the world I'd do without you, Jackie."

"I pray everyday they find a cure for it."

"Yes, Lord. Sugar disease is an awful thing to live with. My heart really goes out to people who live alone. I'm so grateful for your help, honey. I just couldn't see sticking myself with a needle."

I packed away the supplies. "What do you miss the most?"

"About what?"

"About your life before you had diabetes..."

"When I was about your age, me and your Daddy used to go fishing together in a creek. We'd sit side-by-side, reaching in the bucket for worms and–"

"Ugh, Mama. You touched worms?"

She smiled and her whole face lit up. "Ummhmm. You can't catch fish without bait."

"But weren't they nasty and slimy?"

"It was all worth it to catch a nice perch or whiting. He'd gut the fish and I'd take it home and fry 'em with my mama's batter recipe. She'd stand by the stove, watching me to make sure I wasn't messing up. But no matter how many times she offered to help, I insisted on doing everything on my own. I wanted your father to know that I was gifted in the kitchen. And boy oh boy, we'd have some good eating. Those were real special times."

"Did you love Daddy, even way back then?"

"Of course so."

"But isn't fifteen too young to feel love?"

"That depends, honey. What I felt for your father when I was a girl was more like puppy love."

"But your parents let you go on dates together and you and Daddy won't let me–"

"For the record, young lady, fishing at the creek *wasn't* a date. Your father and I never went alone. My brother and his cousin always tagged along." She lifted her eyebrows. "What's the meaning of all of these questions anyhow? Does this have anything to do with that Roger boy?"

"No, Mama."

"Are you sure?"

"I don't like Roger. Not one bit."

"Remember what I told you about boys?"

"Keep your legs closed and your panties up."

"That's right."

"You don't have to worry about me and Roger."

"Jackie, if you ever feel those urges inside of you to do something that you know you shouldn't be doing, you've got to have enough self-control to fight it. Now that you're getting older, you're going to spend more and more time trying to keep the devil at bay."

"Mama, I don't like Roger. Not at all."

"Sometimes, I worry about you, being friends with that Diane girl...she's on the fast side and her mama is too. I just don't want anything to happen to you."

"Nothing's gonna happen, Mama and Diane's not fast."

"I saw that outfit she was wearing the other day when she came over here. Girls who dress like that are inviting all types of trouble."

Daddy unlocked the front door and walked inside holding a bag of groceries.

"You need me to help unload the rest?" I stood up quickly, anxious for any excuse to end my conversation with Mama. There was so much she didn't understand.

"Sure, sweetheart. Bring in the bag with the ice cream first. I don't want it to melt."

I grinned. "You got ice cream? What kind?"

"Your favorite, of course."

"Thanks, Daddy."

"Don't thank me, thank the Lord. He's the one who made everything possible from the ice cream to the collard greens!"

***

It was the first day of vacation Bible school. I sat in the chapel with all of the other children. Being close to him made me nervous. My heart was beating really fast. My underarms were sweating too. It was already hot enough in there. The ceiling fans spinning around in the air did nothing to cool the room.

All of the kids waited for my father to deliver the starting day prayer. He was busy talking to the church secretary, Sister Sadie. From the serious looks on their faces, it seemed important. She handed him some paperwork.

I sat next to Camille. She wore pink-framed glasses. Her hair was in a short afro (even though afros really weren't in style anymore.) But we had something in common because her mother dressed her the same way Mama dressed me. Both Camille and I had bodies shapely enough to strut our stuff on *Soul Train,* but the world would never know it.

"Want some?" She smacked her chewing gum and made a small, purple bubble.

"You're gonna get us in trouble. You know it's against the rules to have that in here."

"It's grape. You like grape?"

"Who doesn't like grape?"

I stuck out my hand. She put a square of the Bubblicious gum in my palm.

"Thanks." I opened it slowly and popped it into my mouth.

"So are you happy that school is out or what?"

I nodded. "I get to spend more time with my boyfriend."

"I don't even know why you like him. Roger is way cuter."

"Then you can have Roger."

"He doesn't like me. He's all about you."

"Roger has a big ole hook head."

"My older brother used to have a head like that too, but he doesn't anymore."

"Well, what if you marry Roger and y'all have a whole bunch of babies and they all have little hook heads?"

"Shut up."

Suddenly, I felt his eyes on me. I looked at him across the room.

Camille noticed us staring at each other. "Uugghh..."

"You're just jealous of me and my man. When you get one, you'll find out about all the stuff you're missing."

"Like what?"

"Like what it feels like to be kissed so good you never want it to stop..." I whispered in her ear.

"You're so nasty. I'm gonna tell Reverend Foster on you."

"Go ahead. It's not like he's gonna believe you."

Daddy stood at the podium. "Young people, it's wonderful to see you here this morning. I know the summertime is a time when many of you want to go outside and play. But for some young people who don't have the guidance that you've been blessed with, this is the season for all sorts of trouble. There are gangs for boys and a whole different kind of mischief for girls.

"But we don't have to worry about that with any of you, because you made the choice to be in God's house. Amen! So as we begin our first day of vacation Bible school, I expect you all to be on your best behavior. Every moment that you're here, please set a Christian example. If you have a buddy who is going down the wrong track, do what you can to help him or her get back on the right one.

"I want you to listen to me, Reverend Moore, Reverend Watkins, Deacon Leonard, Brother Mitchell, Sister Yolanda, Sister Sadie and especially Sister Maple because she's the one who is preparing our meals. Amen! All of us are here to help you learn and grow in one capacity or the other. You can use this education in the Bible to build a foundation to achieve any goal. If you want to be a doctor, a lawyer, or even the president, you can make it happen so long as you hold on to God's unchanging hand.

"I'd like to ask for all of you to bow your heads... Heavenly Father, we came to you today with humble hearts. We ask for your anointing as we begin our first day of vacation Bible school. Help us all to learn and enjoy positive Christian fellowship. We ask these blessings in the name of Your son, Jesus Christ. Amen.

"Now, I want all of the boys to line up behind Reverend Moore and I want the girls to line up behind Sister Yolanda."

As Camille and I moved toward Sister Yolanda, I walked by him. I watched him standing there with the boys. He touched his right eyebrow twice. I got so excited because that was his signal that he wanted to meet me in our secret place.

Camille rolled her eyes. She spoke under her breath, "I can't believe you actually like him."

"And I can't believe you actually like Roger."

She whispered, "How can you kiss Reverend Moore?"

"His name is Darnell. I don't call him reverend anything."

"It's still gross no matter what you call him."

"Come on, girls!" Sister Yolanda waved us closer. "All of you beautiful young women are first and foremost children of God. I want you to say it with me...I am a child of God..."

"I am a child of God," I said in unison with Camille and the rest of the girls.

"Good. I am so happy that I'm going to be spending the summer with you. Reverend Moore and I take this work very seriously. We're going to study the Lord's words together and engage in open dialogue about how to apply those principles to everyday life. Like I said, this is serious work, but I still expect for us to enjoy the journey along the way.

"So as you know, Reverend Moore is leading the boys and I am leading the girls. He is also my husband and in our marriage we believe in following Christ and having fun too. So we're going to have a few challenges where the girls and boys will face off. Whichever team knows the most about the Bible at the end the summer will be rewarded with a dinner downtown at Fishbone's at the end of the summer."

One girl smiled and hollered out, "Ooohhh, I'm gonna tear up them fried shrimp!"

"That's the spirit. I already told Reverend Moore that our team is going to win, so let's prove me right! Follow me, girls!" Sister Yolanda led us out of the chapel.

"Your boyfriend's wife is so nice," Camille whispered.

"Darnell is gonna divorce her when I graduate from high school."

"Whatever, girl. The only thing on my mind is going to Fishbone's."

Jackie

THIRTEEN
August 9, 1978

I looked up and down the hallway to make sure no one was around as I made my way to the meeting room. My heart was racing. I knew I was only minutes away from being alone with Darnell. I quietly unlocked the door with the key he gave me.

Inside, there was a long wooden table and several chairs. After service every Sunday, Daddy and all of the trustees met in there to count the tithes and discuss church business. But during the week, the room was a hide-a-way for me and the man I loved.

I locked the door behind me just like he told me to. Usually, I let Darnell undress me. But this time, I wanted to be sexy for him.

I didn't want him to look at me and see a little girl. I took my hair out of its ponytail. Then, I unbuttoned my blouse and slipped out of my plaid skirt.

I finger combed my hair so that it fell down past my

shoulders like Jayne Kennedy's did when she talked about football players on TV. I felt like a grown woman. I couldn't see my reflection, but in my mind, I could see Darnell's smile. I was excited about what he was going to say to me and do to me.

Mama and Daddy taught me that what I was doing with Darnell was a sin because we weren't married. But I knew we were going to get married one day. He promised me.

In many ways, he already felt like my husband. Every time we were together he always told me he loved me.

As I waited for him, I thought about how our relationship started. I had a crush on Darnell from the day he became the associate pastor at our church two years ago.

From his bright hazel eyes to his dimpled smile, he was the finest guy I'd ever seen. His wife didn't deserve him.

Sister Yolanda was an average-looking woman with a flat nose. On top of that, she was bowlegged too. But some people claimed she was pretty just because she was light-skinned. They needed their eyes checked!

When I started the ninth grade at Cass Tech, Darnell said, "You have to be really smart to get into that school. You have definitely been blessed with intelligence *and* a beautiful appearance."

I kept thinking about what he said over and over again. Most grown-ups said I was pretty when they complimented my looks, but Darnell thought I was *beautiful!* I wrote three pages about it in my diary that night.

A few months later, he came over to our house for dinner. Sister Yolanda was unable to come with him because she was picking up her cousins at the airport. Daddy and I cooked smothered chicken, rice, green beans and candied yams. Since Mama's leg was bothering her, she didn't sit at the dinner table with us. She ate her dinner on a TV tray in front of the couch.

After some Neapolitan ice cream for dessert, I took the dirty bowls and spoons into the kitchen. As I started washing the dishes, I heard Daddy and Darnell laughing. The sound of the running water made it hard to hear their whole conversation, but I was pretty sure that Darnell said, "You have a lovely daughter, Reverend Foster."

"Jackie has always been a sweet child."

"And I know that when the time comes, she's going to have fellas lined up at your doorstep."

"Not before I get my shotgun first." Daddy chuckled.

"Amen, brother." He laughed.

Soon afterward, Darnell said he had to leave. Daddy and I walked him to the door. Darnell thanked us for dinner.

"Abe!" Mama called out from the living room.

"I'll be right there," Daddy said. "I'd better go check in on her. I'll see you at Bible study on Wednesday.

Jackie, you lock up, okay?"

The moment Daddy walked away, Darnell asked, "Did you really cook the candied yams and the green beans all by yourself?"

"Yes, sir."

"Do I look old enough to be a sir?"

I shrugged. "How old are you?"

Darnell smiled. "Why?"

"Because…"

"Because what?"

"Just tell me."

"I'm twenty-seven."

"That's old."

"That depends… Well, young lady, I've got to get going. I'll see you later." He opened his arms and I walked into his embrace. It felt good to wrapped up in his strong arms. I took in the smell of his cologne. We held onto each other for much longer than normal hug. As he pulled away, his lips brushed against my neck. I looked up at his face, wondering if he did it on purpose or by accident.

He whispered. "Did you like that?"

I blushed and nodded. I was in too much shock to speak. I liked a guy and he liked me too! That had never happened before.

As the months passed, Darnell and I tried more things together but we were always careful. He told me never to tell anybody or we would both be in a lot of trouble. I kept that promise for the most part. The secret was too big and exciting to keep it all to myself. I only told Diane and I trusted her with my life. I also told Camille, but she didn't have any friends besides me so I didn't have to worry about her telling either.

Now, I slid my left bra strap down my shoulder, anticipating Darnell's touch. He always knew how to make me feel so good. I looked forward to the day when we would live together in the same house as husband and wife. I knew it was going to be hard for our families to accept it at first, but they would come around. God wants everyone to be happy and Darnell makes me very happy.

I heard keys jingling at the door. Then, Daddy said, "Lord help me! This can't be happening!"

Darnell said, "Reverend Foster, please..."

I snatched my clothes off the floor, hurried into the closet and shut the door behind me.

They walked inside. Someone turned on the light.

"I warned you this man had the devil in him," Deacon Leonard said. "I knew it from the day he came here and the way he made eyes at everything wearing a skirt. But for the life of me, I don't understand why you had to go and mess with Jackie. That's just sick."

"Is this true? Did you take advantage of my baby girl?"

"Reverend Foster, I...I don't want you to take this the wrong way, but she's the one who initiated–"

"How could you even shape your mouth to say a thing like that? She ain't but a child!"

"I realize that. But my flesh got the best of me. There's only so much temptation a man can stand before–"

"Get out of my sight and never come back here!"

"Can we please talk this out. I know you're a reasonable man, Reverend Foster and the Bible teaches us the power of forgiveness–"

"You'd best leave right now before I do something that I really regret. I am a man of faith, but if I have to look at you for another second, I'm not sure what I might do."

I heard Darnell walk out. Tears slid down my cheeks. I thought that he was going to tell them that he loved me, but I was disappointed that he told lies to make me seem like some nasty girl.

How could he say *I* initiated it? He was the one who kissed me first and told me it was okay because we were in love.

I looked around the closet for something I could turn into a noose. Killing myself seemed easier than facing the world again.

"Lord help me, I could kill him," Daddy said. "What kind of man would… Well, I'm gonna take Jackie down to the police station to file charges. I want to see that fool thrown under the jail for what's he's done. And to think, if it hadn't been for that Camille girl coming forward to Sister Sadie, I would have never found out about any of this."

"I can only imagine how terrible you feel right now," Deacon Leonard said. "As you know, I've got three girls of my own and if any man laid a hand on them, suffice to say that turning the other cheek would be out of the question. That said, you really need to think this thing through…"

"What are you talking about?"

"There's no need for you to press charges. That so-called reverend will never step foot in this place again. Chances are, he'll leave town."

"What does that have to do with him paying for what he did to my baby girl?"

"You've got to do what you think is best, Reverend Foster, as a father and as a man. But as the pastor of the church, you need to consider this…a trial about a child being molested would shine a bad light on New Kingdom Baptist. Membership is already down as it is. The bottom line is that families wouldn't feel comfortable worshiping here and rightfully so."

"Are you really suggesting that I let him get away with it?"

"No, like I said, you've got to do what you think is right. But hasn't Jackie already been through enough? Do you really want to put her through the stress of testifying in front of a jury about every godforsaken thing that snake did to her? You know those testimonies can get quite detailed. Everything, and I mean everything would come out."

"I still think..."

"You want to see your daughter's reputation ruined?"

"Of course not, but..."

"Getting the police involved would only put a scarlet letter on Jackie. No trial is gonna change what happened. And what if he was acquitted? You heard those terrible things he said about her? You know how these things work. The girl is always the one who's at fault. The jury might believe him."

"No, they couldn't, she's a child."

"Yes, but she's fifteen. I know she's your baby girl, but unfortunately, there are some people who might have a different point of view. Reverend Foster, I have a great deal of respect for you and I'm telling you this as a friend, I think it would be for the best if we dealt with this matter privately. Not many people know about what happened and it's for the best if it stays that way."

"I don't know..." Daddy took a deep breath. "I'm gonna have to pray on this really hard."

"You do that, reverend. And you know I'm here to help in any capacity."

"I appreciate that."

***

I stayed in the closet for hours after they left. I never wanted to come out of there. I was angry at myself for telling Camille.

If she hadn't opened her big mouth, my secret would

still be safe. Now, the man I loved was gone and my life was forever changed.

Jackie

FOURTEEN
January 20, 1979

I woke up to the sound of Jack Johnson III crowing.
Aunt Rose told me that he came from a long line
of fierce roosters. The noises in Mississippi were so
different than the ones I was used to back in Detroit.
There were mooing cows and chirping crickets instead
of car horns and gunshots.

I pulled back my lace curtain and saw the orange sun
rising in the distance. I took my time getting out of bed.
My big, round belly made me move slower than Mama.
I put on my robe and followed the smell of grits, bacon
and biscuits into the kitchen. Aunt Rose was standing at
the stove.

I yawned. "Good morning, Aunt Rose."

"Hey, honey!" She turned around. Her short, black
hair was wrapped up in rollers. She had the same dark
skin color as Daddy but her eyes were light brown. Aunt
Rose was a tall, thin woman with long arms and big

feet. She always teased that she'd never found a husband because there wasn't a man around who could fill her shoes.

"How'd you sleep?"

"I had to wake up four times to pee. Other than that, fine I guess."

She smiled. "Well, it won't be long. The baby will be here anyday."

I sat down at the table. "I'm scared, Aunt Rose."

"Why's that?"

"What if my baby doesn't love me?"

"Hush girl, where'd you get such a foolish idea?"

"What if...the baby is mad at me for sinning?"

She walked over and put her hand on my shoulder. "It doesn't matter how a child comes into the world, every child is a gift from God. And there is nothing more pure than the love between a mother and a child. So long as you love your baby, your baby is gonna love you. Do you love your baby?"

"Yes, ma'am."

"Then, rest assured, your baby can feel your love right now, this very second. Now, let me fix you a plate because we can't have no hungry babies up in this house."

I smiled. "Thanks, Aunt Rose."

I gobbled up every bite of my breakfast. Then, Aunt Rose and I went into the living room. I sat down on the couch. She didn't have a TV, but she had a radio that was as big as a dresser. She turned the dial to a blues station.

Muddy Waters sang "Got My Mojo Working" as she opened her sewing kit.

She handed me some blue fabric and a pattern. "You get started on that in case it's a boy. And I'm gonna make a dress in case it's a girl."

"Aunt Rose?"

"Yes, honey."

"Do you mind if we switch? I wanna make the dress. I really, really hope it's a girl."

"I know. But no matter if God gives you a girl or boy, you've got to love that child just the same."

"I will."

She handed me the pink fabric and the pattern.

"Thank you."

"Don't mention it." She took the blue fabric and the pattern and made her way to the rocking chair. She hummed along with Muddy Waters and rocked back and forth as she threaded a needle. Aunt Rose was such a good seamstress that she got it on the first try.

I unraveled a bit of my thread and wet the tip in my mouth. I'd discovered the miracle of spit! Unlike Aunt Rose, I couldn't thread without it. I held the needle up to the window's light. It still took me a minute and half to thread it, but I was proud of myself.

When I came here six months ago, I poked my fingers more than the fabric. It took a lot of patience and Band-Aids, but now I could almost make anything. I was sure that I could even make my own wedding gown, but I knew for sure that I wouldn't be marrying Darnell.

After that day I stood in the closet, listening to my life fall apart, things got worse. Mama and Daddy looked at me like they didn't love me anymore. They never said it with their mouths, but they said it with their eyes.

Then, one morning I woke up feeling like I had food poisoning. I threw up so much for so long that I thought I'd be stuck in the bathroom for days. Daddy knocked on the door and asked me what was wrong. Before I knew it, he bust open the door. Daddy had the same look in his eyes like he did on the night he found out his younger brother was killed in a car accident.

"Lord, please don't let it be true!" He shouted so loud that it scared me.

Daddy told me to get dressed and took me to the clinic. A short nurse with a blonde wig asked me to pee in a cup. Half an hour later, a doctor told me I was pregnant. I cried on Daddy's shoulder as the doctor spoke about my "options."

A.) Have an abortion. (But I couldn't imagine killing my baby.)
B.) "Place the baby up for adoption." (But I couldn't imagine that either.)
C.) Raise the child on my own. (But that was an option Mama and Daddy would never agree to.)

Everybody looked down on teenage mothers, but the

one I knew of was a good person. Peaches lived three blocks over. She was sixteen when she had her son. I remember watching her push her baby up to the park and hearing some of the neighbors calling her nasty names, especially the boys. One of them said that she opened her legs on any day for any reason.

But everybody with eyes could see that her baby was loved. Little Dwayne was always smiling. Of course he didn't have any teeth so his face was all gums and dimples and there was a lot of drool too. But a baby wouldn't smile like that if something was wrong.

On the drive back from the doctor's office, Daddy said, "You'll have to take a semester off of school. I'll talk to Aunt Rose and see if you can stay with her till the baby is born. After that, we'll see about putting the child up for adoption and you can come back home."

"I'm not going to Mississippi and I'm not giving up my baby!"

"Under the circumstances, this is for the best."

"You're only sending me away because you and Mama are so sanctified and righteous that y'all are too ashamed to have me around!"

"Watch your mouth, young lady! As God as my witness, you'd better not ever speak to me like that again!"

Daddy looked at me like he was going to hit me. My heart pounded. I looked down. "Sorry, Daddy."

***

Now, I sat in Aunt Rose's living room, sewing clothes

for my baby. The baby that I was willing to do anything to keep.

"How is it coming along?"

I weaved the needle through the pink fabric. "Good. Still not as good as yours though."

"Oh, you'll be better than me in due time."

"You think so?"

"Mmmmhmmm. You've got a special knack for this." She grabbed a second needle from the pin cushion. "I sure am glad to be doing this, honey. I just love making baby clothes. It's probably because the Lord never blessed me with a child of my own."

"Why?"

"The pickings are mighty slim in these parts. I couldn't find nobody worth marrying."

Blood rushed to my cheeks. I thought of how I was about to have a baby without a husband or even a boyfriend.

"I didn't mean nothing by it, honey. You ain't got nothing to be ashamed of. It's like I told you, every child is a gift from God."

"Since you never had a husband, does that mean that you never...you know...did it?"

"Now, now, don't go meddlin' in grown folks' business." She hummed along with Billie Holiday's "God Bless The Child." "Isn't this just one of the prettiest songs you ever heard, doesn't it just reach deep inside and touch your soul..."

"Aunt Rose, Aunt Rose!"

"What is it?"

I stood up. I was wet from the waist down. "I'm so sorry, I tried to make it to the bathroom, but it came out of nowhere…"

"Oh my, it looks like your water broke!" Aunt Rose's eyes got wide. "I'd better call the midwife."

***

I was in labor for eighteen hours. It hurt so bad that my voice gave out from all the screaming by the time the baby was born. But the second the midwife put my daughter in my arms, it was like God cut off a switch and the pain stopped. I started crying. She was so pretty, like a doll baby, my very own doll baby. I kissed her forehead and her cheeks. I told her I loved her and she looked up at me as if she was saying, "I love you too, Mama."

***

A week later, I was in my bedroom, sleeping with my baby girl on my chest. Then, I heard Daddy's voice in the living room.

"Where's Jackie and the baby?"

"Resting," Aunt Rose said. "They both still wore out."

"Well, I need you to wake them up. If we get going now, I can make it to Memphis before it gets dark."

"You ought to just stay here for the night. Looks to me like you could use some rest yourself."

"I'll be fine. Just make me some coffee."

"You sure? I got ham hocks and corn pone, fried okra too."

"It sounds real good, but we can get us something to eat in Memphis. They got plenty of restaurants there."

"Abe, I was thinking...what if Jackie and the baby stayed with me a little longer?"

"She's got to get back to her school."

"Maybe she could go to a high school here."

"Jackie attends one of the best high schools in the city. Her home is with me and her mama in Detroit."

"What you're asking her to do is no easy thing. Why don't you let her stay with me the rest of the school year and start back next September?"

"Everyday she spends with that baby is a day that she's gonna wanna keep it. I only want what's best for her, you've got to understand that. It's all been decided. I promised her mama that I was gonna bring her back home and that's what I intend on doing. There's no talking me out of it."

"Well, if it's all the same to you, do you mind staying here tonight? I'd like the chance to give my niece and my great-niece a proper goodbye and one last home-cooked dinner for the road."

"All right."

"I appreciate it, Abe. It's been wonderful having Jackie here. I'd welcome her back anytime."

"I'm sure she'd love to come back and visit, under different circumstances of course."

"Before you up and got religion, you used to be more understanding."

"God calls on us to mimic only His son. And I strive to be like Christ, even though I may fall short sometimes."

"I hear you. All I ask is that you give Jackie a chance. One mistake doesn't define a whole life."

"I know that. It's just been hard on our family. I don't know why in the world she did what she did."

Aunt Rose laughed. "Now, you're pulling my chain. Is this coming from the same man who used to run off in the cornfields with Wilma Jean? How old were you back then? If I remember it correctly you were fourteen, a full year younger than Jackie before she–"

"I was a boy! That's different. Besides, that all happened before I got saved."

"Mmmhmm. Whatever you say, *Reverend* Foster."

"See now, this is exactly the reason why I didn't want to stay for dinner. You could never keep your mouth shut." He chuckled. "Ain't no wonder why you stayed single all these years."

Aunt Rose laughed. "I'd rather be all by my lonesome than miserable and married any day."

***

The next morning, I gave Aunt Rose an extra-long goodbye hug. I was going to miss her so much. She had been good to me during the hardest days of my life. I held my baby close to my chest as I walked toward Daddy's Lincoln. He opened the door and I hesitated before getting inside. Part of me wanted to run back up to Aunt Rose's porch and stay forever, but I knew Daddy wasn't having it. So, I got inside slowly.

We drove for nearly an hour without speaking. Finally, he said, "She sure is a pretty sight. What's the name you picked out again?"

"Princess."

"What kind of name is that?"

"You know the singer, Prince?"

"You talking about the one who wears his hair like a girl and performs heathen music?"

"His real name is Prince. It's on his birth certificate and everything. So if he can be Prince, I thought I can name my baby Princess. Princess Foster. She sounds famous already, doesn't she?"

"You needn't worry about such foolish things. All that matters is that the child has a relationship with God." He paused. "I've got some good news, your mama and I changed our mind about putting the baby up for adoption."

I smiled. "Thank you, Daddy."

"Your mama and I have decided that we will raise the child as our own."

"But you can't! This is my baby!"

"What kind of life are capable of providing for this child? You don't have a husband, a job or so much as a high school diploma. Let me and your mama give this baby a stable home. I realize this hurts you. If you love her as much as I know you do, you'll do what's best. In a few years, when you get married, you can have a child of your own, the right way. In the mean time, you've got to trust me and your mama, sweetheart."

***

Two weeks later, my baby was baptized as Rhonda Michelle Foster. It wasn't that hard to convince people that Mama was her mother. Because of her size, she looked big enough to be pregnant. Daddy told everyone that Mama went to the hospital with stomach cramps and discovered that she was in labor with a surprise baby.

It was so painful to watch my child grow up and call another woman "Mama" that I decided to get as far away from my family as possible. When I graduated from high school, I got a full scholarship to the University of Connecticut. I was so glad to be seven hundred miles away from home. I never wanted to come back.

Rhonda

FIFTEEN

Finding a job turned out to be the only thing harder than staying sober. I tried Monster.com, CareerBuilder. com and a bunch of other ones. I went to the individual websites for companies like Home Depot, Staples and even McDonald's. Sometimes, I spent hours online filling out one application. My eyes were strained from staring at the computer screen all day. The questions gave me a headache.

Which elementary school did you attend?

Describe yourself in three words:

What was your proudest achievement?

I wanted type in a question of my own:

What does any of this have to do with operating a register or mopping a floor?

I set a goal for myself: one application a day, no matter what. Most of the times, I filled out two. But none of the companies bothered to email or call me. Not one! Daddy saw how frustrated I was and he said, "You can't get your foot in the door without knowing somebody on the inside."

I knew he was right, but I didn't want Daddy to get involved because he had been rescuing me my whole life. He tried to convince me that there was no shame in accepting help, but I still told him no. One day, he clapped his hands and sang "Lean On Me." He changed the lyrics a little; *"You just call on me, sister, when you need a hand. We all need somebody to lean on..."*

After I finished laughing, (Daddy's singing voice was pretty bad) I gave up my stubborn ways. Daddy called Mrs. Vernon, the facility director of Hope Senior Village. It was an assisted living home run by our sister church, Eternal Light Baptist Church. When he told her about my qualifications, she agreed to bring me in for an interview.

I was so nervous, but I was more confident than usual because I had on a new suit and my hair was freshly done. My stylist had given me layered curls with reddish-brown highlights. My hair was so healthy and thick that strangers probably thought I was wearing a wig. Best of all, the lady at the Macy's makeup counter showed me how to put on my foundation to make my skin look normal. I felt more beautiful again.

When Mrs. Vernon asked me why I'd been out of work for so many years, I explained, "At first, I stayed home to care for my son after he was born. My husband had a successful business at the time and we were able to afford it. But then...I...I'm sure Daddy has talked to you about my problems..."

"No, Reverend Foster didn't tell me much of anything besides the fact that you're his daughter and you used to work at Providence Hospital."

"Well, I don't want to lie to you, ma'am. I was addicted to drugs. I've been clean for a few months now, but it makes no difference how long I stay clean, I'll always be an addict. But now, I am on a path to become a better person. And I hope that as I get better, I can make other people's lives better, if you give me a chance. But I can understand if you don't want to hire me."

"I didn't say—"

"Well, I said it for you. Mrs. Vernon, please don't just give me this job because you're doing my father some kind of favor. I only want to work here if you think I'm the right fit."

"Rhonda, you have been very honest with me and now it's my turn to be honest with you... I gave you this job interview as a favor to Reverend Foster and I was on the fence about hiring you until just now. There is nothing that I value more in an employee than honesty and I would like to welcome you to our family here at Hope Senior Village."

I thanked God as I stood up to shake her hand. That night, Daddy took me to dinner at Red Lobster's to celebrate. As I stuffed my face with cheddar-baked biscuits, I couldn't believe how much my life had turned around. A few months ago, I was strung out in a crack house with the likes of Ratman, now I was starting a new job.

Working gave me a real sense of purpose. I just loved waking up every morning and putting on my scrubs. I was so grateful to help people in need and earn a bit of money to cover my child support payments and legal fees. Each payday brought me closer to seeing Antoine again. Even though Jaimaya refused to return my phone calls, I kept hoping that she would give me another chance. I felt I deserved it. I'd been sober for six months, one week, three days and counting.

***

I pushed a food cart down the hall. It was my fifth week on the job and I was getting to know everybody. I waved at the nurses behind the desk. For now, I was an orderly, but I planned to finish up my community college classes to become a RN. I wanted to be an example to my kids that anything was possible with faith and hard work.

I rolled my cart into room number 317. My heart felt sad as I walked past the empty bed. Mrs. Wellington, the patient who used to be Mrs. Hill's roommate passed away last week. Even though I only knew her for a month, I became attached to her. She was a sweet old lady who used to sing "Go Tell It On The Mountain" so beautifully that it made my eyes water.

Mrs. Wellington lived to be ninety-nine years old. Everyone agreed that she enjoyed a full and blessed life, but I still grieved for her. I felt really sorry that she missed her hundredth birthday by only three months. But Daddy always said, "You never know when the Lord will call you home, so do right by Him and you'll never have to worry." All I could do was spend my time trying to earn God's forgiveness so that I would be ready on judgment day.

I brought the cart toward Mrs. Hill's bed. "Good afternoon, ma'am."

"How are you today, young lady?" The wrinkles on her brown face deepened as she grinned at me. Her face was framed by kinky, silver hair.

"I'm blessed. How are you?"

"Well, I'm blessed too. Blessed *and* hungry. What you got there?"

"Something you'll like." I helped her sit up in bed. I put the plate on her tray and slid it closer to her.

"What is it?"

"I've got your favorite today." I took the lid off of her lunch plate.

She frowned at the three mashed-lumps. I couldn't

blame her. The meal didn't look very appetizing because it was puréed.

I put on a big smile to help cheer her up. "Let's see here...we got cauliflower, corn and baked beans! Nurse Maria told me that you love cauliflower. Isn't that right?"

She pointed with her slightly curved index finger (Mrs. Hill's arthritis was so bad she couldn't lay her hands completely flat.) "I know cauliflower when I see it and that there ain't no cauliflower!"

I spooned up a little bit. "Why don't you just taste it? If you don't like it, I'll see about getting you something else to eat."

She flashed her toothless smile. "How 'bout some ribs?"

"I can't promise ribs, but I'll see what I can do." I brought the spoon up to her mouth. "But first, could you please try a little?"

She took a small bite. "It is cauliflower!"

"See, I told you. I wouldn't lie to you for nothing in this world."

"President Nixon lied. And you best believe I ain't gonna vote for what's-his-face on election day...Ford. No way! He's guilty by association. My mama taught me that if you lie down with dogs, you bound to get fleas! But his wife, Betty, she's all right with me. It took a lot of courage for her to tell the whole world she had breast cancer. She said it right in *Time* magazine. I held onto that issue. In my day, women kept quiet about that sort of thing." She swallowed a bit more food and asked, "The election is next Tuesday, right?"

"No, ma'am. The election already passed. We got a black president now."

She laughed. "You ought not tease me about such a thing. Ain't no way this country would ever allow a Negro in the White House, at least not until the year 3000!"

I filled up a spoon with more cauliflower and fed her. "Well, it already did happen and he was elected twice. His name is Barack Obama."

"Ba-who what?" She paused. "You know who should be the president right now? Shirley Chisholm. I was so proud when she ran. She's unbought and unbossed! When was that? I think it was four or five years ago, back in '72. Mmmhmm. Yep. It was '72. I cried when she lost, but there was a part of me that was relieved. I was so scared that the Klan was gonna get to her. Can you imagine a Negro woman as president? Now, that would really be something."

"It might happen someday soon... You want to try some of the baked beans?"

"Naw."

"What about some creamed corn?"

"Did you read about what Mayor Young said to them nosy reporters the other day. It was front-page news. He told them they could kiss 'em where the sun don't shine. Of course, that's not exactly what he said. I'm a

Christian woman, so I'm not gonna quote the man. But he sure can cuss, can't he?"

"We have a white mayor now."

"Naw, we voted Gibbs out back in '73. Mayor Young might be high yellow, but he ain't white."

"Mayor Young passed away years ago. Now, we have Mayor Duggan."

"Girl, you talking crazy. You're telling me that America has a black president and Detroit has a white mayor? Chile, you must be coming down with a fever."

"Mrs. Hill–"

"And you know what George Bush said? 'Read my lips: no new taxes.'" She laughed. "But I tell you what, that young man, Clinton, has potential and it don't hurt that he's easy on the eyes."

I spooned up some of the corn. "Will you eat a little more, please?"

She opened her mouth and swallowed. "I'm really looking forward to the revival next month. They'll be plenty of good eating there! Miss Maple is gonna bake her famous lemon pound cake. Negroes come all the way from the west side for a slice! And Miss Maple makes everything from scratch...she don't fool with no Betty Crocker mix. These young girls is lazy in the kitchen nowadays, everything they cook comes out of a can or a box or a frozen bag. It's no wonder why the divorce rate is so high."

"You're doing good, ma'am," I said. "If you eat a

few more bites I'll see about getting you some dessert."

"If it ain't Miss Maple's lemon pound cake, don't even bother." She swallowed a bit. "I tell you one thing, I can't wait to see Reverend Foster and Reverend Cook preach the Lord's word. Our churches have been hosting that double revival for coming up on ten years now."

"More like forty-five years..."

"It ain't been nowhere near that long, honey."

"Mrs. Hill, do you remember when I told you yesterday that the year is 2014?"

She chuckled. "What is it that President Reagan always says... 'Trust but verify.' I don't see eye-to-eye on him with much of anything, but I do agree with that one, trust but verify." She stared at my face. "You sure got your share of those Foster genes, but I still think you look more like your father."

"My father *is* Reverend Foster."

"Honey, there's nothing to be ashamed of. I understand. The man who raised me wasn't my real daddy, but I called him Papa all the same."

"Come on, let's finish up your lunch." I decided not to correct her. Mrs. Hill's dementia left her confused about everything from the current year to the current president. Now, she was confused about Daddy.

I knew that Abe Foster was my biological father just as sure as I had given birth to Jaimaya and Antoine. When I was a teenager, I remember hearing that Daddy had a baby outside his marriage. According to the rumor, I was that baby and Mama forgave him on the condition that she could raise me as her own child. Mama's health was so bad that I thought it might be true. To me, it didn't matter one way or the other. No one except God was perfect.

In Daddy's younger years, he was a very handsome looking man. The women of the church clung to every word of his sermon, especially Sister Sadie. Sometimes, I looked at her and wondered if she might be my real mother, but I never questioned for one second that Daddy was my real father.

Jackie

SIXTEEN

I put my grocery bags down on the welcome mat and unlocked my apartment door. I was so excited to prepare a home cooked meal for Harold tonight. I'd picked up all the ingredients for seafood jambalaya. I also bought a sweet potato pie from the bakery. I looked forward to our romantic, candlelit dinner.

We had been together for almost six months. Harold and I shared a deep connection. He was the first man I ever told that Rhonda was my biological daughter and not my sister. He was also the first man I had dated for so long without being intimate.

I respected his wishes for us not to have relations before marriage, but there were times when I felt overwhelmed with passion for him. One kiss from his soft lips sent me to ecstasy. I'd never been so attracted to anyone and it was much more than a physical thing. We were bound emotionally and spiritually too. "Equally yoked" as Daddy would say.

I heard the buzzing sound of the television as I walked inside with my grocery bags. I made a mental note to myself to turn off my appliances when I wasn't home. I needed to watch my electricity bill along with all of my other bills. I wasn't making *Soul Beat* money anymore.

Maintaining a robust rainy day fund had been a big priority since I got laid off years ago and I watched most of my possessions disappear one-by-one. Despite my relative job security at Center Stage Studios, I had learned to never take my finances for granted.

"Hey, sexy, what's for dinner?" Patrick sat with his feet propped up on my couch, sipping a Heineken. There was a large, black suitcase on wheels lying across my rug.

"What are you doing here?"

"Instead of boring you with all of the details, how about the abbreviated version: Honey, I'm home!"

"I should have changed my locks, but I never thought that you would actually come back."

"This isn't the reaction I anticipated."

"Get out!"

He took a long swig of beer and stood up. "Hold on for a sec, can we please have a discussion like mature adults... First, let me begin by saying that you were right about Ebony. If I could do it all over again, I would have never left you. It was a mistake. Arguably one of the biggest mistakes of my life. I know that we might have a rocky re-adjustment period, but we can make it work. If you give me another chance–"

"I told you to get out. We have nothing to discuss."

"Please don't put me out. If you do, I'll have to sleep in my office or go to my mama's house. What's that gonna look like at my age? Come on, Jackie! I know I messed up really bad and I can't imagine how much I let you down. But we had something really special."

"That's right. *Had,* as in past tense. I didn't realize it at the time, but when you hurt me, you actually did me a favor."

"Huh?" He looked at the golden cross chain around my neck. "What's that?"

"A gift from my boyfriend."

"Let me get this straight…you got so desperate that you started dating some holy roller?" He chuckled. "I never figured you for the type, Jackie."

"Don't you dare disrespect God or the man I love!"

"Wow, look at you. A preacher's daughter through and through."

"Get out, Patrick or else I'm calling the police!" I unzipped my purse and took out my cell phone.

"Calm down! I'm leaving, okay?" He grabbed his suitcase and walked toward the door. "Just tell me something, Jackie…"

"What?"

"Do you really love this man or is he just somebody to fill the void I caused?"

"Diane was right."

"What does she have to do with anything?"

"The problem with our relationship was that it had no spiritual base. Now that I know what it's like to be loved the right way, I can never go back to a man like you. But I don't have any hard feelings. In fact, I'm going to pray for you as soon as you get up out of here."

"Call me when you come to your senses." He opened the door. Then, he turned around and looked into my eyes for a long while. Finally, he left.

My heart felt relieved as I made my way to the kitchen. If Patrick had been waiting for me in my apartment a few weeks after we broke up, I would have taken him back without explanations or demands. But now, I had Harold's love and too much respect for myself to ever go back down that road again. I was proud of the woman I had become and I was sure that God was proud of me too.

***

After filling our bellies with dinner and dessert, Harold and I sat together on my living room couch. He grinned. "That food was amazing!"

"Thank you."

"I could get used to eating like this everyday."

"Oh really?"

He nodded. "And you know what else I appreciate about you besides your culinary genius?"

"What's that?"

"You never held back the truth from me. I know it

wasn't easy for you to tell me about Rhonda. And you even told me about what Patrick did today. A lot of women would have kept that to themselves."

"Well, the locksmith was here when you walked in, so I knew that would raise questions. But I still would have told you about his surprise visit either way. A relationship can't function on secrets and lies."

"Your honesty is so beautiful to me, Jackie."

"Is that the only thing that's beautiful about me?"

He caressed my face with his finger tips. "It would take me a lifetime to list everything that's beautiful about you."

I blushed. "You're such a charmer."

"No, I'm just trying to be like you. Honest. And I can honestly say that you're the most beautiful woman I've ever loved, both inside and out."

"Wow, Harold, I don't really know what to say–"

He kissed me. "Just say you'll love me for the rest of your life."

"Harold, um...if I'm going to be honest, there's something else about my past that I think you should know."

"Why do you look so serious all the sudden?" He flashed a nervous smile. "You're not on the 'America's Most Wanted' list, are you?"

"What I'm about to tell you, I haven't discussed with anybody. Not my family, not even Diane."

"Well, if you're ready to share, I'm ready to listen."

"I want to show you something. I'll be right back."

"Okay."

I went into my bedroom and took my scrapbook out of a box in my closet. When I walked back into the living room, Harold looked up at me with an anxious expression. I sat next to him and opened the scrapbook to the center page. Inside, there was a letter.

***

April 12, 1979

My Dearest Jackie Marie,

Let me begin by saying that having you and baby Princess here was the happiest time of my life. (I know your parents named her Rhonda, but I still like Princess better.) You are such a beautiful girl and I am so proud of you. No matter what, I never want you to feel shame in your heart. My biggest hope for you is that you will go after all of your dreams and never forget how to do a proper double stitch.

I fell ill a few weeks ago. When I went to the doctor, I found out I had colon cancer. It started in my liver and it spread to my whole body. He says I don't have much longer to live. It could be matter of days before I am gone. There's nothing much that can be done. Please don't feel sorry for me. I've made my peace with the Lord.

I thought long and hard before writing you this letter. There were so many times when I wanted to tell you face-to-face while you were here. I just didn't have the courage to do it and I was afraid at how you would react to the news. I prayed on it and God spoke to my heart. I came to the conclusion that it wouldn't be right for me to go to my grave without you knowing the truth.

I have been lying to everybody for years about not having any children. I had two babies. The first one was a boy. He died during childbirth. My heart broke up into a thousand little pieces. I stayed in bed for days, crying and holding my dead son in my arms. I was just sixteen when he was born. I thought I would never get over the pain of losing him. Then, a three years later, I got pregnant again.

I gave birth to a baby girl that I named Pauline after your grandmother. She was healthy and beautiful with a head full of hair. My boyfriend was so happy. His name was Morris Cunningham. We planned to get married as soon as he got home from Vietnam. But Morris came back from the war in a pine box. It felt like I couldn't breathe when I saw his body in that casket. I was devastated that God took away my first-born son and my future husband.

I got so blue inside that I would go for days and days without eating. My mother ended up taking care of Baby

Pauline for the most part. Folks in the community told me that I needed to just snap out of it. Believe me when I tell you that I tried. I wanted to be there for my baby girl, but I just couldn't.

When your parents came to visit that Christmas and saw how bad off I was, they offered to take Baby Pauline up north with them for awhile until I felt better. My mother thought it would be a good idea, especially since they couldn't have any children of their own. So I agreed to let them take Baby Pauline, but I had every intention of getting her back one day.

A few months passed and I felt better. I called Abe and told him I was going to take the Greyhound bus to Detroit to get my baby. He told me that they loved my Baby Pauline like she was their own and it would be wrong to take her back now. Then, your mother got on the phone and she broke down crying saying that she couldn't go on living without the baby.

I felt so bad about the situation that I agreed to let them keep my baby. I thought I was doing the right thing at the time. I missed my child with everything inside of me but I knew they would give her a good home.

As the years passed, I started to regret it. My mother encouraged me to find someone and start a new family of my own, but I just couldn't get over my love for Baby Pauline. I turned down all my marriage proposals and lived out the rest of my days alone.

Your parents agreed to take you in under the condition that I keep the truth to myself. I still want you to know that I will always love you, Pauline. I wish everyday that I could have been a mother to you. Isn't it sad that we both made the same choice. I gave you up the same way you gave up Baby Princess. If I could have turned back time, I would have insisted that Abe let you and my granddaughter stay with me.

I hope you don't hate me for what I did and all the things I didn't do. I pray that you can forgive me one day. My only dying wish is that you please don't tell your father what I told you. I know it would break Abe's heart.

Love your mother,

Rose

***

"As soon as I got this letter, I hurried to the train station and bought a ticket to Mississippi." I wiped away the tears from my eyes. "I never told my parents where I was going. They thought I ran away. I didn't even call

Aunt Rose to tell her I was on my way down there. There were things I wanted to tell her that I just couldn't say on the phone.

"By the time I made it down there, she was in the hospital. She was so weak and drugged up that she barely recognized me. She'd lost so much weight, I barely recognized her. I stayed by her bedside day and night. She slept most of the times. But one day, she opened her eyes. She was suddenly lucid. She reached out for my hand and said, 'My daughter came back to me. I love you, baby.' A few days after that...she was gone..."

Harold held me as I cried into his shoulder. He rubbed my back. "You are a very strong woman, just like your mother. I know Rose is looking down on you from heaven right now."

"I just wish...I could have known her better." I sobbed.

"You'll always have her in your heart."

"There was a part of me that knew it all along, especially when I spent all those months with her down in Mississippi..."

"My cousin went through a similar situation. He found out from a family friend that the woman he knew as his mother was really his aunt. It messed him up pretty bad. But he felt better after he confronted the family about it. He waited till the reunion and then, he said his piece."

"What happened?"

"It was rough. There was a lot of shouting followed

by a lot of tears, but in the end, my cousin felt so much better. My whole family did too. I guess what I'm saying is…I think you should have a conversation with your father and Rhonda to get all of this out in the open."

"I can't…"

"I don't think you can afford not to. Holding on to all of this isn't healthy."

"It's not as easy as you're making it sound."

He took my hands into his. "Could you please at least pray on it."

I took a deep breath. "I will."

Rhonda

SEVENTEEN

I sat at a table in the staff kitchen. I unwrapped the saran wrap from around my turkey sandwich and took a bite. Then, I reached into my bag of Better Made potato chips and popped a few into my mouth. I washed it down with some Faygo cola.

Unlike some of my co-workers who had their food delivered from the pizza and sub restaurant next door, I woke up early every morning to pack my lunch. I was determined to save as much money as possible for my legal battle with Nate. I counted down the days until I could see my son again. As for Jaimaya, she still hadn't returned my calls. But yesterday, she sent a text that read: *"I'll call you this weekend. BTW, how is Grandpa?"*

I texted her back: *"Great! I look forward to your call. Grandpa is fine. What does BTW mean?"*

Although Jaimaya didn't reply, a young co-worker explained to me that BTW meant "by the way." I still had a long way to go when it came to texting shorthand.

The only thing I knew for sure was LOL stood for "laugh out loud."

The kitchen door swung open and a tall man in a janitor's uniform walked inside. He looked to be about 6'4. He wasn't a bad looking man. His height and his cheekbones were his most attractive features. Mama would have said that he had Indian in his family.

He smiled at my lunch. "I see you've got two Detroit originals there...Faygo and Better Made! But how can you drink Faygo cola? I'm all about that grape. I can get down with some red too. Maybe a little pineapple. But cola? Come on, girl."

"It's actually pretty good."

He poured himself a cup of coffee. "By the way, I'm Omar."

"BTW, I'm Rhonda."

"BTW?"

"It stands for 'by the way.' Don't you text?"

"Naw. That's what got Kwame Kilpatrick all caught up. He wouldn't be locked up now if it wasn't for them text messages."

I laughed.

"How long you been working here?" He sipped his coffee.

My phone buzzed with a new voicemail. "Excuse me." I played the message.

"Rhonda, this is Attorney Reed. I just wanted to give you an update on your case. To summarize it in a nutshell, Nate's lawyer is playing hardball. But please don't get discouraged. We can't give in, we've got to fight harder. You still have solid legal standing as Antoine's mother...it just might take a little longer than I expected to resolve this. Please call me when you can and I'll fill you in on the details. Take care, bye."

I hung up the phone with tears in my eyes.

"What's wrong?"

"Nothing."

Omar sat across from me. "I'm not leaving till you tell me what's going on."

"It's none of your business, okay!"

"Girl, you must be a lifelong eastsider with attitude like that." He chuckled.

"Could you just leave me alone."

"I'm sorry. I didn't mean to joke with you. I was just trying to get you to smile. You've got a real pretty smile."

I rolled my eyes.

He walked to the door. "It was nice meeting you, Rhonda. I'll see you around."

As soon as he left, I buried my head into my hands and sobbed. I wondered if I would ever see Antoine again.

***

I carried a small tray with a cup of water and a container of multicolored pills. I walked into room number 317. Mrs. Hill was wide-awake, watching Dr. Phil on TV.

"Hey there, young lady." She grinned.

"It's time to take your medicine." I wasn't in the smiling mood. All I could think about was Attorney Reed's message.

"What station does Donahue come on?"

"His show was canceled years ago, Mrs. Hill." I put the tray down.

"No, that can't be right."

"His show was canceled, okay? Can you please take your pills now?"

"They just can't cancel the man's show like that. Naw. And who's this bald-headed fella who thinks he knows all the answers? This doesn't make a bit of sense! Why replace Donahue with the likes of him?"

"Open up, Mrs. Hill."

"Huh?"

"Like this...aahhhhh!"

She slowly opened her mouth. I carefully inserted the small pill.

"Now, drink some of this." I held the cup to her lips.

She swallowed some water.

"Now, stick out your tongue."

"That's just rude. My mama taught me better than to do that."

"I need to check and make sure you took the pill."

She shook her head.

"Could you please stick out your tongue, Mrs. Hill."

"I will do no such thing. No such thing!"

"We go through this everyday and I'm always patient with you. But right now, I really need you to cooperate with me."

"No!"

"Please."

"Something ain't right. Just what's the matter with you anyway?"

"I'm fine."

"You ain't foolin' nobody, Geraldine. I know that you're good and tired of waking up before dawn to catch the bus downtown. And all day long, you go about cooking and cleaning with an empty heart because you miss your own babies. I know it's killing you to be apart from them. It must be strange to get paid to look after somebody else's children while you can't be with your own. But you won't have to do this forever. As soon as Lester gets one of them factory jobs, you can hang up your maid's uniform and spend all your time with your babies. In the meantime, your babies will be waiting on you. They know Mama's coming home soon."

I started to cry. Despite or maybe because of her dementia, Mrs. Hill could sense how much I missed my children.

She patted my shoulder. "Remember this, honey... trouble don't last always. You hear?"

"Yes, ma'am."

***

Outside, the September rain was falling hard and

steady. I waited for Daddy by the employee entrance. He was running a little late picking me up because Bible study had gone into overtime. That happened more often than not. Whenever Daddy got into a conversation about God's word, he could talk for hours.

I looked out of the small window by the exit door to see if his car was approaching. There was no sign of Daddy's Lincoln, but I got my umbrella ready. I was anxious to get home and talk to Attorney Reed. I didn't feel comfortable calling him from work. I was afraid that the news might be so emotional that I couldn't function on the job. His voicemail had been bad enough. I felt terrible about the way I treated Mrs. Hill earlier that day.

"Hey, Rhonda!"

I turned around and saw Omar zipping up his jacket.

"Are you still mad at me?"

"The way I acted had nothing to do with you."

"Well, I'd still like to make it up to you sometime... Are you waiting on somebody?"

"Yeah."

"Where do you stay?"

"Off of Outer Drive and 7 Mile."

"I could take you home, I drive right past there."

"No thanks."

"My bad. You're probably up here waiting on your boyfriend or husband and I don't want you to think I'm trying to get fresh with you or anything... I'm just trying to be friendly, that's all."

"Hold on a minute." I took my cell phone out my purse and called Daddy.

He answered on the fourth ring. "Hello?"

"Hey, Daddy, have you left the church yet?"

"I'll be leaving in five minutes."

"That's okay, one of my co-workers offered to give me a ride home."

"Are you sure? It's no trouble for me to pick you up. I can be there in twenty minutes, half an hour tops."

"It's okay, Daddy. I'll see you when you get home. I love you."

"I love you too, sweetheart."

I hung up and looked up at Omar. "Well, I'm ready when you are."

"Let me pull my van up to the door so you won't have to walk in the rain."

"A little water won't hurt me."

"No, you stay right here. My mama raised me better than that."

I watched out the window as Omar ran to his dark green Dodge Caravan. There were several dents and scratches on the body of the vehicle. It looked to be at least fifteen years old. I said a silent prayer that we could it make back to my house without the van breaking down.

Omar pulled up to the doorway. I popped my umbrella and hurried toward the van. He reached over and opened the passenger door. He held my hand as I climbed inside.

"Thanks," I said.

"Don't mention it."

He turned on the radio to the classic R&B station. Debra Laws and Ronnie Laws sang "Very Special."

"That sure don't make music like this anymore. See, I'm old school. Class of '85. How about you?"

"Class of '96."

"Oh."

"I know I look older."

"No, it's not that. You just have a mature vibe going on."

"Thanks." I smiled. I appreciated Omar's kind recovery.

"You mind getting me some gum out the glove box? I've got to keep my grill minty fresh. You never know when you might get lucky and share a kiss with a fine woman and if I was to get lucky I know she wouldn't want a brotha with stank breath."

I smiled. It had been ages since a man genuinely flirted with me. Even though Omar wasn't really my type, I appreciated the attention. I grinned as I opened the glove box and spotted a box of Trident next to a bag of marijuana.

"Oh, my bad. I didn't mean for you to see that. Please don't tell nobody at work."

My smile faded. "I won't." I handed him a piece of gum.

"You can help yourself to some if you want."

"Are you talking about the Trident or the–"

"Either one."

I ached to get high. After what my attorney told me, I needed something to lift my spirits. But somehow, I found the strength to say, "No thanks."

A few minutes later, he pulled in front of Daddy's house on Kenmoore Street. "Thanks for the ride."

"Don't mention it, I can bring you home anytime."

"I...um..."

"What is it?"

"How much would you charge me to...if I wanted to..."

Omar reached over and opened his glove box. He put the bag of marijuana in my lap. "Consider it a gift."

"Thanks." I put the bag in my purse. "I want you to know that I don't normally do this, it's just that I had a really bad day."

"Well, it looks like it's about to get a whole lot better."

"Yeah, this is just what I need right now." I opened the car door and climbed out. "I'll see you tomorrow."

"No doubt. Take it easy, Rhonda. That there is pure chronic. I was planning on enjoying that tonight, but I'm hookin' you up 'cause I like you."

I smiled. "Thanks."

As I made my way up the wet sidewalk, I was relieved to see that Daddy's car wasn't parked in the driveway. When I got inside the house, I called him. His phone went to voicemail. At the sound of the beep, I said, "Hey,

Daddy, I hope you get this message in time. If it's not too much trouble, could you please pick me up some Chips Ahoy cookies from the store? Thanks, I really appreciate it. I love you."

I hurried to my bedroom. I shut the door behind me and cracked open the window. Then, I stuffed a towel underneath the door. I opened up the bag of weed and rolled myself a joint. My hands started shaking as I picked up my lighter.

Even though marijuana wasn't a hard drug, I was still seconds away from getting high. I thought about the pact I made with God on the night Ratman tried to rape me. I looked up to heaven and thought, *"Lord, please help me! I don't wanna do this…"*

I heard Daddy's footsteps in the hallway. "Rhonda?"

"Yeah…"

"I got your cookies."

"I'm just changing out of my work clothes. I'll be out in a minute…"

"Well, I put them on the table, okay?"

As soon as I heard him walk away, I grabbed the marijuana and headed to the bathroom. I closed the door behind me. I opened the bag and poured all of the weed into the toilet bowl. I watched the green leaves swirl around the bowl as I flushed.

I was very grateful that God had sent another angel to save me from myself. That day at the mall, it was an old lady in sneakers. This time, it was Daddy. Next time…I promised myself that there could never be a next time.

I knew that I had to find a healthier way to deal with my pain. My mind went back in time to the beginning of my sadness...

Rhonda

EIGHTEEN
July 17, 1984

I wanted to play outside with Sam, Keisha and Pookie, but I was stuck in the house because Daddy said he needed to talk to me. A serious talk, he said. It was really, really hot in the living room. It was so hot that I thought that I was going to melt right into the floor like Evilene in *The Wiz*. But I wasn't mean like her, so I didn't think God would let that happen to me.

Daddy sat next to me on the couch. "There are going to be some changes around the house. It might take some getting used to at first, but...I want you to know that Sister Laura and I are engaged."

"What does that mean, Daddy?"

"It means she's going to come live with us after we get married."

"Why?"

He took a deep breath. "Your mother was called to heaven over a year and half ago. And now that your sister's away at college...don't you think it gets lonely around here sometimes?"

"No."

"You're too young to understand it right now, but the good Lord intended for every man to have a wife."

"Then you should marry Sister Sadie! She's really nice. She can live with us as long as you still cook everything. I'm not trying to be mean but her food makes my belly hurt."

He laughed. "Sister Sadie is a very sweet woman, but I don't have those sort of feelings for her."

"But you can't marry Sister Laura!"

"Why not?"

"Because I don't like her."

"Why not?"

I shrugged. When Mama died, the women at church came over to the house with all kinds of food. Some of them brought my favorite, macaroni and cheese! But one day, I heard Sister Laura say she didn't like macaroni and cheese. If she didn't like my favorite food in the whole wide world, then I didn't like her.

"Daddy..." I started crying because I was scared that I was never, ever going to eat macaroni and cheese again.

"What is it, sweetheart?"

The doorbell went "ding-dong!"

"I think that's Sister Laura." He looked at me. "Now, I want you to wipe away those tears because the three of us are going out for ice cream."

I smiled. "Really? You're the best daddy ever!"

"Thank you, sweetheart."

***

At the Dairy Queen, we sat at a white table with a red umbrella. I licked my chocolate and vanilla swirl ice cream cone with rainbow sprinkles. Sister Laura ate her plain vanilla ice cream out of a bowl with a spoon. Daddy sipped a large Coke. He couldn't eat anything with milk in it because it upset his tummy.

Sister Laura was dressed strange to me. It was burning hot and she was wearing a really long, black dress that covered up her legs and arms. She even had on stockings! All of the other women and girls wore shorts.

"You ought to slow down. It's not lady like to eat so fast. Isn't that right, Abe?"

Daddy nodded.

"Sorry, ma'am."

"From now on, you should just call me Mama."

"It might be a little soon for all of that."

I was happy Daddy said something because Sister Laura was never, ever going to be my mama.

"I'm so sorry, dear. I didn't mean to overstep. I apologize."

"Now, go ahead and tell Sister Laura that you accept her apology."

"I accept....your apology."

"It's going to take some time for the three of us to get used to each other, but I know that our family will be a

177

happy one. As long as we all keep God first, then we'll get along just fine."

Sister Laura put her hand on Daddy's shoulder. "This means so much to me. I've always wanted a family of my own and now, I feel so blessed to have finally found one."

Sister Laura smiled at me and I smiled back at her because she had a pretty smile. All of her teeth were perfect, shiny and really white. "I realize I can never take the place of your mama but it is my hope that you will accept me into your heart as a mother figure."

"What does mother figure mean?"

"It means someone who is like a second mama."

"Okay. You can be my second mama."

She frowned.

"What's the matter, Laura?"

"Oh, my, would you look at that." She pointed at two girls ordering ice cream. They had on short shorts and tank tops. They looked like they were old enough to be in high school. "A pair Mary Magdalenes in the making! It's a disgrace that their parents allowed them to leave the house in those clothes. I would have tied them up and beat the devil out of them."

"Thank the Lord we never have to worry about Rhonda dressing like that."

"Amen to that!"

***

A month later, Daddy and Sister Laura got married at the church. She wore a long, white dress and Daddy put on a black suit. Since I was the flower girl, I got to throw rose petals down the aisle.

I was so pretty. I had on a brand new dress and my hair was pressed and curled. We ate dinner in the basement. Everybody kept saying congratulations to Daddy and Sister Laura. I was so glad because I got to eat two slices of cake and drink four cups of Sister Maple's homemade punch.

But the happy times stopped after Sister Laura moved into our house. First, she told me that I couldn't watch my cartoons because they were sacrilegious. I didn't understand what that meant, but I missed laughing at Elmer Fudd chase Bugs Bunny on Saturday mornings.

Sister Laura wouldn't allow me go outside and play with my friends. She said they came from broken homes and they were a bad influence on me. I didn't understand what that meant either. I would look out the window and watch Pookie, Sam and Keisha riding their bikes and yell out to them. But they never heard me. I got so sad that I cried.

Sister Laura read the Bible out loud a lot. She made me listen. She said that it was important that I learn all of God's word by heart if I wanted to go to heaven. I tried my best, but the "thees" and "therefores" got confusing. I was afraid that I was going to hell at six years old.

One day, Daddy left out and said he was coming back with a big surprise for me. Most of the times, his surprise was ice cream. Sometimes, it was something even better like a Barbie doll. I was so excited thinking about what it might be.

Sister Sadie was in the kitchen making some lunch. I was alone in my room, so I came up with a make believe game. I pretended to be Jackie. Her bed was right next to my bed, but she only slept there when she came to visit from college. Since Jackie didn't come home a lot, it was mostly empty. I missed my big sister. People at church told me I looked just like her. I hoped they were right. I wanted to be just like her, on the inside and the outside.

I put on her prom dress. It was way too big for me, but I still liked it because it was gold and shiny. Jackie looked so pretty when she went to her prom. I was only two years old, so I didn't remember it. But I looked at Jackie's prom pictures all the time. Her boyfriend was cute with curly hair. I wished I had a boyfriend too. I only had a friend-boy and since Sister Laura didn't let me play with Sam anymore, I was pretty sure that he was Keisha's friend-boy now.

I smiled at myself in the tall mirror as I put on some of Jackie's lipstick. Then, I put on her high heel shoes. I walked around the room singing and dancing. *"I'm so pretty. Look at me. I'm so pretty. Look at me. I'm–"*

"What in God's name…" Sister Laura stood in the doorway. I was so scared because I didn't even hear her open the door. She had a really mean look in her eyes. Whenever she looked at me like that, it meant that she was going to hit me. She only hurt me when Daddy wasn't around. I never told him about it because Sister Laura said that God would make me pay if I did.

"I'm just make-believing that I'm Jackie."

She ran up to me and grabbed my arms until they hurt so bad that I thought they would fall off. I screamed and cried.

"You should never aspire to be like her! She's nothing but a whore! You hear me?"

"Don't call my sister bad words." I didn't know what *whore* meant, but she said the word like she was spitting.

She slapped my face hard. "You will learn not to talk back to me!" She smiled. But her smile wasn't pretty anymore like it was on that day at Dairy Queen. Her smile made me afraid now. "Since you want to follow in your sister's footsteps, here's what we'll do. First, I want you to get naked just like she did."

"No!"

"Do it!" She stood back and folded her arms.

I took off Jackie's prom dress.

"Take off everything!"

I pulled my panties down. She grabbed me by the arm and put me in the closet. She closed the door. I stood there, crying in the dark.

"Please...I'm so...sorry...please let me out."

"Not until you've learned your lesson."

"Please..." I tried to open the door, but I couldn't. "Please!"

"You're old enough to find out what happens to

young girls who disobey God. Although you might not realize it now, I'm actually helping you. If it wasn't for me, you would become just like Jackie. I'm not going to let that happen. With my guidance, you will grow up to be a decent Christian young woman. But you must listen to me and obey me just like I am God."

"Can you please, please let me out…"

"Don't interrupt me!"

I cried harder. "Please! I'll do anything you say, please, just let me out!"

"Not yet."

"I have to go to the bathroom."

"Young lady, have you forgotten that it's a sin to lie?"

"But I really have to go!"

"The devil is…"

I peed on the floor.

"Lord help me! You are behaving like some zoo animal."

"Please let me out…"

"No, I'm going to leave you in there with your filth."

I heard my sister yell, "Oh my God!"

"Jackie!" I yelled.

"I would advise you not to come any closer. Nobody, especially not you, is going to stop me from keeping this child out of the devil's reach."

"Let my sister out of that closet, right now!"

"I am doing the Lord's work and I told you to step back! Don't touch me, you dirty whore!"

I couldn't see anything, but I could tell they were fighting by the sounds they made. I didn't just want Jackie to win. I wanted her to hurt Sister Laura as bad as she had hurt me. There was a really loud noise. Jackie screamed. I was scared that my sister was losing. I heard Jackie crying.

I heard Daddy's voice in the hallway say, "Rhonda? How do you like the surprise of your big sister coming home for a visit?"

"Daddy! Daddy!" I screamed.

He yelled, "Lord help me! What have you done?"

"Calm down, Abe. With all do respect, we both know Jackie's history and what she's capable of. Rest assured, I was only defending myself."

"Don't you say another word!"

"You ought to be thanking me for trying to instill some Christian values in your wayward children."

"What you've done isn't Christian at all. It's evil! And I want you out of my house!"

"Abe, can we just talk–"

"I told you to get out!"

"Okay, I'll leave for now to let you cool off, but I'm not giving up on us, Abe. You're the husband God intended for me."

"Leave or God help me, I will... you need to leave right now!"

The closet door opened. Daddy stood there. He looked at me with sad eyes. He went to the drawer and got a clean towel. He wrapped it around me and picked me up in his arms. He rocked me like I was a baby and said, "I'm so sorry, sweetheart. I had no idea that she…"

Jackie was sitting on the floor. There was blood on the side of her face. I looked down and saw my lamp on the floor. It was broken. I felt so sad for Jackie. I could tell that she was in a lot of pain. The only good thing was that Sister Laura was gone and I prayed she was never coming back.

Daddy held me as he sat down next to Jackie. He started to cry. "Girls, I'm so sorry that I didn't see the truth about Laura sooner. I'm so sorry. I know I let you down." He took off his glasses and wiped his eyes. "Jackie, we'd better get you to the hospital and let the doctors take a look at you. I can't believe what she did. Most of all, I can't believe I had such evil right under my roof. Lord help me!"

***

Jackie ended up getting four stitches on her jaw. Later that night, I asked her if she was mad at me because I was the reason that she had to fight Sister Laura. She said, "I'm always going to look out for you, you're my baby."

"You mean your baby sister?"

"Yep, that's right. Let's try to go to sleep, okay?"

I closed my eyes. I had a dream that Jackie, Mama and I were living together inside of a rainbow with Barbie dolls and My Little Ponies. It made me so happy that I forgot all about how sad Sister Laura used to make me feel.

Jackie

NINETEEN

As I drove down Kenmoore Street, I smiled at the Mrs. B's extravagant Halloween decorations. There were plastic witches and ghosts in her front yard. She had four carved pumpkins on her porch and a giant Frankenstein poster on her front door.

When I was a kid, I looked forward to putting on my costume and going to Mrs. B's house. She always gave out the best candy on the block. Now, she lived in one of the few occupied houses in the neighborhood. So much had changed over the years. But some things seemed permanent, like the sight of Daddy's old blue Lincoln in his driveway after church.

I parked behind him and got out of my car. I pressed the button on my key fob to set my alarm and walked up to the front porch. Even though I had a key, I decided to ring the doorbell.

Daddy opened the door. "Hey, sweetheart. It's so good to see you."

We hugged.

"So, I see you finally decided to join us for Sunday dinner."

I walked inside to the smell of roast beef. The delicious spices made my stomach grumble.

"The food will be ready in about half an hour. Why don't you come sit with me and your sister. We're watching that TV show, *Thicker Than Water.* Have you ever heard of it?"

"No." I followed him into the living room.

"It's a reality show about a preacher and his family. At first, I didn't think I'd like it, but it's growing on me. They're all about sticking together. Any family that can stick together and keep God first is just fine in my book."

"Hey, Jackie!" Rhonda grinned at me.

I gave her a big hug. "Hey!" I sat down next to her on the couch.

"It's so good to see both of my girls together." Daddy sat down in his easy chair.

Rhonda turned to me. "Where have you been, stranger?"

"Working. Speaking of work, how are things at your job?"

"Everything's going good and I'll be taking my nursing classes when the winter semester starts at WC3."

"I'm happy to hear that."

Daddy pointed at the TV and laughed. "Church folk can be a trip sometimes!"

I picked up the remote off of the coffee table and turned the TV off.

Rhonda frowned. "What'd you do that for?"

I swallowed. "I've been praying a lot lately...and I...I'm tired of living with all these secrets."

He shook his head. "There's a right way and a wrong way to go about things and what you're doing is wrong," Daddy said. "The things that happened in the past belong in the past."

"Aren't you sick of the lies too, Daddy? Or are you more concerned about keeping up your Christian appearances?"

"Don't talk to Daddy like that! What did he ever do to you except try to love you? The only thing I can think of is that you must still be mad about Sister Laura. Daddy admitted he made a mistake when he married her and I forgave him for that years ago. It's time for you to do the same thing."

"Daddy has been apologizing his whole life when he should have been protecting us. Every time I look in the mirror, I'm reminded of what happened, what that woman did to me. But the saddest part of is that that's not even the worst of it." I looked at him. "And you know exactly what I'm talking about."

Daddy stood up. "I'm not gonna have any parts of this. You come in my house stirring up all of this mess. You ought to be ashamed of yourself."

"I used to be ashamed, but for the first time in my

life, I'm not ashamed anymore. If you are really the Christian man you claim to be then why haven't you told Rhonda the truth?"

Daddy said, "I love you, sweetheart. I always have and I always will. There's nothing you can say or do that will change that. I'm happy to hear that you are praying again and working on your relationship with God. But you have yet to walk a mile or even one step in my shoes!"

"But, Daddy–"

"Your sister is just now getting some stability in her life and here you come dredging up pieces of the past that don't even matter anymore."

"But–"

"I wish I could make you understand, sweetheart. I come from a generation where people didn't need to know everything about everything. When I was seventeen, I heard through the grapevine that the man who raised me wasn't my blood father. I never told him that I knew the truth. It didn't make a bit of difference to me. In my eyes, Herbert Foster is and will forever be my papa. I'm thankful that the Lord blessed me with such a fine father. Good parents aren't just the folks who bring you in the world, they are the ones who love you and teach you how to make something of yourself."

"What is this all about, Daddy?" Rhonda asked.

"I'm through talking about it." He walked into the kitchen.

"See! You've gone an upset him. What's wrong with

you? You know he's got high blood pressure."

I followed Daddy.

"Haven't you bothered him enough already?" Rhonda walked behind us.

"Daddy," I said.

He turned around. He was stirring rice on the stovetop.

"I just wanted to tell you that I'm sorry… What I did was disrespectful and I hope you can accept my apology. I didn't mean to…I'm sorry, Daddy."

"It's all right, sweetheart."

"Are you sure you're not mad at me?"

"I couldn't be mad at you for nothing in this world."

"I love you, Daddy." I wrapped my arm around him.

He smiled. "I love you too, sweetheart. Now, let's eat!"

"I don't think I'm gonna stay for dinner."

"Why not?"

"Well, I'm…cutting back on red meat," I lied. Daddy's roast was amazing, but I couldn't bring myself to sit at the dinner table with them after my failed attempt at an honest conversation. It was disappointing to see that my real life was nothing like a movie with a happily ever after ending.

"Oh."

"I think I'd better get going."

"Girl, you don't know what you're missing. This here roast is a thing of beauty!"

"I can tell, Daddy. But I think I'll pass."

"Will you be here next Sunday?"

"Yeah, I'll try to make it. I'd like to introduce you to my boyfriend."

"I'm looking forward to it."

"Me too." Rhonda grinned.

***

As soon as I got home, I called Harold.

"Hey, beautiful," he said.

"Hey, handsome."

"See, there you go."

"What?"

"You have an affect on me like no other woman."

"Oh really?"

"I've told you that before, but I guess you don't mind me repeating myself."

I smiled. "Not when it comes to that."

"So how did everything go with your father and Rhonda?"

"Not the way I planned."

"What happened?"

"Daddy basically refused to talk about it and I didn't want to press the issue."

"Do you plan to talk to them again?"

"I don't think so. I think I'd better leave it alone."

"But you told me–"

"I know what I said before, but I guess I've had a change of heart. Maybe the truth is overrated."

"Please don't say that."

"I love my father more than I care about the truth."

"You shouldn't have to choose, Jackie. I think it would help if you prayed with Reverend Foster and maybe–"

"My father is seventy-eight years old. He deserves to live out the rest of his life in peace."

"Well, you have to do what feels right in your heart. You know I support you no matter what."

"I appreciate that. It's just…"

"What is it?"

"I think about Rhonda too. If I was her, I'd want to know the truth, but I just can't put Daddy through that."

"Are you sure you're making the right decision?"

"Yeah. It's the right decision for now."

"I understand."

"Do you think less of me?"

"Of course not. I love you, Jackie. I know this isn't easy for you."

"I love you too. This has been such an overwhelming day for me. I need a little time to sort through my emotions. But I promise to call you before I go to bed."

"Okay, I love you too."

I hung up the phone and took a deep breath. Even though Harold wasn't disappointed in me, I was still disappointed in myself. I was torn about confronting Daddy and Rhonda with the truth. My father seemed determined to leave well enough alone and I didn't want to hurt him. On the other hand, the secrets and lies of my past made me weary. I got down on my knees and prayed to God for a sign.

Rhonda

TWENTY

I walked behind the members of the congregation as I entered the chapel. New Kingdom Baptist Church was a place filled with familiar sights and faces. The smiles of the long-time parishioners and the sunlight shining through the stained glass windows made me feel at home.

I was wearing my new green skirt suit. My hair was tied back into a bun. I wore Mama's pearl necklace around my neck. I felt beautiful on the inside and the outside. I had been sober for eight months. I was proud of the woman I'd become.

At work, I'd kept away from Omar and his temptations. Instead, I focused on making a difference in the lives of the seniors I cared for everyday. Jaimaya and Antoine were the only things missing in my life. I loved my children so much. My world was incomplete without them.

"Good morning, dear. This is truly a day the Lord has made." Sister Velma handed me a program. She was a gray-haired woman with a wide smile. She'd been an usher at our church for over thirty years.

"Amen to that." I took the program. "Thank you, Sister Velma."

"You're looking very nice today."

"Thanks, but I can't hold a candle to you."

She smiled. "Aw hush, chile."

I giggled.

"I'll tell you what...one of these days, I'd like to introduce you to my nephew. He's single and right around your age."

"I appreciate that, but–"

"There's nothing wrong with making a new friend, right? You never know, the right friend could turn out to be sent from above."

"But–"

"We'll talk after service." She patted my shoulder.

"Yes, ma'am." I nodded. There was no use in arguing with Sister Velma. But I was nowhere near ready to open my heart to another man again. After the nightmares I survived with my two ex-husbands, I was content to be alone. All I needed was God and my children. I thought of how I used to wake them up every Sunday morning and make pancakes and bacon before coming to hear Daddy preach the Lord's word. I missed those days so much it hurt.

I made my way to my spot in the third pew behind the elders. I'd been listening to my father's sermons from that spot for as long as I could remember. As I looked over, I saw my sister. She was sitting next to a handsome man in a gray suit.

"Hey, Rhonda." Jackie smiled. She opened her arms to me.

"Hey." I hugged her. I was still upset with her for the way she treated Daddy when she came to Sunday dinner last week, but I could never stay mad at her for too long.

She pulled away. "I'd like for you to meet my boyfriend, Harold."

He shook my hand. "It's so nice to meet you. Jackie has told me so much about you."

"Nice to meet you too." I sat down wondering what he knew about my past and my addiction. I turned to Jackie and whispered, "Why did you come here? Is it out of guilt?"

She frowned. "Of course not."

"Do you know how much you upset Daddy? I hope you didn't come here to upset him all over again."

"I just came here to worship."

"You told me that you would never step foot in this church again."

She squeezed my hand. "Things change and so do people, right?"

I nodded, thinking about how much I had changed.

A boy called out, "Mom!" I turned around because he sounded just like my son. The sight of my children walking down the aisle brought tears to my eyes. Jaimaya waddled a few steps behind Antoine. Her belly was swollen with the gift of life. I smiled at the thought that I was going to be a grandmother!

"I missed you both so much!" I stood up and wrapped my arms around Jaimaya and Antoine.

"We missed you too," Antoine said.

"Yeah, Mom," Jaimaya said. "I've been meaning to bring Antoine with me to church for the longest, but I've been busy."

"I can see that." I touched her belly.

"You look really good, Mom."

"Good enough to be a grandma?"

She smiled. "Yeah, in four months."

Jackie stood up and hugged Jaimaya and Antoine. After she introduced them to Harold, we all sat down.

"Mama, can we go out for ice cream after service?" Antoine asked.

Jaimaya blinked. "You want ice cream in November?"

"It's never too cold for Superman ice cream."

I wrapped my arm around his shoulder. "Of course we can go, baby." I thanked the Lord that I was reunited with my beautiful children.

We sat down as the choir sang "I'd Rather Have Jesus."

***

Daddy stood at the podium, looking out over the congregation. He pushed his glasses up on his nose and said, "I'd like everyone to open their Bibles and turn to

First Corinthians, verse thirteen, chapter four and read along with me… Love is patient and kind; love does not envy or boast; it is not arrogant or rude. It does not insist on its own way; it is not irritable or resentful; it does not rejoice at wrongdoing, but rejoices with the truth. Love bears all things, believes all things, hopes all things, endures all things.

"Now, before I delve deeper into God's word this morning, I'd like to share something with you that happened to me the other day… I was in my office, here at church and Sister Sadie knocked on my door. She said, 'Reverend Foster, there's a young man here to see you.'

"As all of you know, I have counseled many church members and non-members through the years. Whether it's a young couple trying to decide if they should get married or a person who is caught up in one of Satan's many traps, I'm always willing to offer a word of advice and prayer. As you know, I've been busy with our Narcotics Anonymous outreach, both here and at other churches. It's a cause that's very close to my heart.

"But people come to me to talk about all types of issues. I'm not one to judge and I always keep my counseling sessions confidential. I've never earned a degree in psychology but I feel called to do this by the Lord Himself. Amen! And I don't need no fancy letters behind my name to help steer folks on the right path.

"So like I was saying before, Sister Sadie told me that there was a young man waiting to see me. I told her to send him right in. He walked into my office and introduced himself. We got into a very serious conversation. I was shocked by what he told me. We held hands and prayed together. And today, is the first time I'm going to share the details of one of my private counseling sessions.

"But before I do that, I want to remind the church that Thanksgiving is a few weeks away and this is that time of year for us to all take inventory of God's bounty. He has given so many blessings that it's easy to discount all that He does for our lives. Some of y'all are so busy complaining about all the things you don't have that you never acknowledge the gifts He has bestowed on you.

"For me, my biggest blessing is my family. Many of you have heard me tell the story about how my wife and I were unable to have children for many years, but then we were blessed with two beautiful daughters. Well, that's the truth. Jackie and Rhonda are my baby girls, even till this day! And I know that my wife is looking down on them proudly from heaven.

"I'd like to go back to that verse in Corinthians again. I know it might seem like I'm a little all over the place this morning, but I want y'all to stay with me. Amen!" He looked down at the Bible and read. "Love is patient and kind; love does not envy or boast; it is not arrogant or rude. It does not insist on its own way; it is not irritable or resentful; it does not rejoice at wrongdoing, but rejoices with the truth. I'm going to stop there. Let's think about that for a minute. *Love rejoices with the truth.*

"All of the years that I've been sharing my family story, I've been telling a half truth. Many of us live with half-truths and even take them to our graves. Sometimes, we tell ourselves that half-truths are okay because the full truth might be too painful or too ugly.

"Up until today, I was one of those people. But today, I stand before you with a different point of view. No matter how ugly or painful the truth might be, the Lord compels us to face it. Running away from the truth makes the devil glad. He wants you to lie. He wants you to pretend. Those are his vices, not the Lord's.

"As many of you know, I will be seventy-nine next month and I don't want to live another day lying to you or myself. Most of all, I choose not to lie to the Lord anymore. My truth is the kind of truth that is common in our community. But today, I'd like to do my part to break those chains.

"It's true that my wife and I were blessed with two beautiful daughters. There is nothing more true than that. Even though Jackie and Rhonda weren't our biological children, it never mattered to us. We still raised them as if they were our own. We loved them so much that we kept that truth from them."

I turned to Jackie, wondering if I was dreaming. Tears fell down her face. She wrapped her arms around me. I started to cry too. I couldn't believe what he was saying. If Daddy wasn't my father, then who was? Jackie rubbed my back gently.

"Jackie was my sister's daughter. My wife and I brought her up here from Mississippi when she was a baby. She brought the happiness back to our home and I will be forever grateful to her for that. My wife and I did our best to give her a good, Christian upbringing rooted in prayer and love.

"But around the time she turned fifteen, the devil threatened to ruin my family. Jackie was molested by a pedophile. This was a man I trusted. I just couldn't believe he would take advantage of my child. Back then, when that sort of thing happened, people had a tendency to blame the girl. They said awful things about my daughter. They called her everything from loose to fast and other things I can't repeat in the Lord's house.

"Looking back at it, I didn't do enough to keep my baby girl safe. It's never, ever the child's fault. I have a lot of regrets about what I did but I have more regrets about what I didn't do. I should have done everything in my power to make sure that sorry excuse for a man was prosecuted to the fullest extent of the law.

"It was a very difficult time for our family. Then, things got even more challenging when we found out that Jackie was pregnant. Although Rhonda came into our lives under unexpected circumstances, we loved her with all our hearts."

Jackie wrapped her arms around me. "I love you, Rhonda. You're my baby girl…"

I pulled away from her and ran down the side aisle

out of the chapel. Jackie followed me into the hallway.

"Is Daddy losing it? What is all of this about?" I dried my eyes with a tissue. It would have been easier for me to believe that my father was suffering from an early onset of Alzheimer's disease than to believe his sermon.

"Yes, I know this a hard way to find out but–"

"All this time, you've been my mother…"

"It's true. I was only fifteen years old when I had you."

"There's this old woman I take care of at my job, Mrs. Hill. She's got dementia really bad and she talks about how Daddy isn't my real father. I didn't want to believe her, but I guess–"

"Mrs. Hill? That was Camille's grandmother."

"Who's Camille?"

"She was one of my closest friends until she opened her mouth about me and the man I thought I was in love with… I hated her at the time. But later on, I came to understand that she was only trying to help me."

"Who is my real father?"

"Darnell Moore…he was…Daddy's assistant pastor. Even though I thought I was grown, I was just a child. It was the biggest mistake of my life except…except for you. When I was pregnant with you, I used to rub my belly and sing to you. I had it in my mind that I was gonna be the best mother in the world to you."

"Then how could you treat me the way you did? All those times I called you and you hung up on me… I know I've made a lot of mistakes, but you shouldn't have turned your back on me like that. God knows I've made my mistakes with Jaimaya and Antoine, but if they ever called me in need, I would never... How could you be so cold to me?"

"I can't tell you how sorry I am. I didn't know how to love you because I didn't know how to love myself. I know that's not an excuse for the way I treated you, but if you give me a chance, I'd like us to make a new start."

"I don't know, Jackie... Everybody has lied to me for all these years about my life. This is a lot for me to take in right now."

"I felt guilty about that everyday. I blamed myself for everything that happened to you. *Everything.* I thought that if you knew the truth, things might have turned out better for you. When I hung up the phone, it was mostly out of shame. I see now that I wasn't ashamed of you, I was really ashamed of myself. I didn't feel comfortable telling you the truth because I knew it would disappoint Daddy and so I carried the secret in my heart for all of these years but now... I just can't do it anymore. I'm sorry you had to find out like this, but I am glad that you finally know. I have always loved you. I never want you to question that."

"I love you too." I hugged her with tears in my eyes.

"We'd better get back in there to hear the rest of Daddy's sermon."

I shook my head. "Naw, I've heard enough truths for

the day." I smiled. "I'm just kidding. To be honest, this isn't all bad news. Today, I found out that my mama is still alive. That is a blessing no matter what."

The congregation stared at us as we made our way to the pew. When we sat down, I felt the glow of my family's love. I looked at Jackie on my left and Antoine and Jaimaya on my right. My heart was so glad.

Daddy cleared his throat. "I thank the good Lord for my daughters everyday. Even though I made mistakes along the way, my greatest joy on this earth was being a father.

"So like I said earlier, that young man and I sat and talked about a great many things. I wanted to share what we talked about. Some of you might have thought he came there to get counseling *from* me, but it turned out that he provided counseling *to* me."

"I want to thank him. What he did took courage and I am a better man for it. He reminded me that my half-truths were doing damage to the people I loved most in the world even though I had convinced myself that I was doing all of us a favor. For years, I have been living with half-truths, but today I am free! My family is free!

"We can live in the truth and I invite all of you to follow that example. An ugly and painful truth is better than a beautiful life. And trust me when I say this...the truth that you think is so ugly and painful might actually turn out to be beautiful if you let the Lord guide your steps. Amen! I'd like the choir to sing 'Our God Is An

Awesome God.'"

As the minister of music played the piano, I cried. Just like Daddy, I felt free in my truth and I was beginning to see the beauty in it.

Jackie

TWENTY-ONE

My emotions were all over the place as I walked down the steps to the church basement. I was overwhelmed, but in a good way. For the first time in decades, my heart felt free again. Harold held my hand as we made our way to my family's table. I smiled at Daddy, Rhonda, Jaimaya, Antoine and Sister Sadie.

"You go ahead and sit next to your father," Sister Sadie said.

"Are you sure?"

"I insist." She stood up.

"Thank you." I sat down next to Daddy. Antoine shifted over to the next chair so that Harold was able to sit next to me. It felt wonderful to be surrounded by all the people who I loved.

"Daddy, I am so proud of what you did today," I said. "I know it wasn't easy for you to get up there in front of the whole congregation and–"

"Like I said in the sermon, I was truly inspired by the

young man who came to my office."

"What exactly did he say?"

Daddy patted my hand. "We discussed quite a few topics…"

Sister Maple walked over to us. "Excuse me, Reverend Foster, I don't mean to interrupt you and your family, but the food is ready to be served."

Daddy winked. "I welcome any interruption that has anything to do with your cooking."

Sister Maple grinned. "Oh, reverend, you're too kind."

"Like I said in the pulpit, I'm just speaking the truth today. Is that barbecue chicken I smell?"

"Yes, reverend."

"Last time, you burnt the barbecue," Sister Sadie mumbled under her breath.

I held in my laughter. Sister Sadie and Sister Maple had competed for Daddy's affection since he divorced that nightmare known as Laura twenty-nine years ago. Sister Maple was gifted in the kitchen and she had round hips. Sister Sadie was an attractive lady who dressed immaculately.

Daddy once teased that he wished he could combine both women to make the ultimate wife. But everybody knew that Sister Sadie had his heart despite Daddy's attempts to keep his personal life private. Life had taught me long ago that secrets never lasted, especially inside of God's house.

"I guess I'd better say a prayer so folks can eat." Daddy stood up and made his way to the center of the room. "Excuse me! Can I have everyone's attention, please?"

The conversations around the room stopped as everyone looked up at my father.

"I am grateful to have all of you here with us on this day that God has made. As you know, here at New Kingdom Baptist, we're all about keeping Christ at the head of our lives and we're all about fellowship. I think it goes without saying that food and fellowship go hand-in-hand. I'd like to thank Sister Maple, Sister Emma and Sister Bernice for preparing a meal for all of us to enjoy. Now, I'd like to ask that we all join hands and bow our hands."

I held Harold's hand and reached across Daddy's empty seat to grab Rhonda's hand. I thought about how there was a time when I feared she was going to die in the streets of an overdose. Knowing that my daughter was healthy and she finally knew the secret I'd been keeping made me feel so grateful. My hands trembled. A tear slid down my cheek before Daddy even started the prayer.

"Heavenly Father, we come before you today in the spirit of thanksgiving. We are humbled by all of the love you have bestowed upon us. We thank you, Lord, for Your son who died for our sins. We thank You for all that You have given us. We thank You for this meal we are about to receive. Please bless the hands that have prepared the food. May this meal nourish our bodies. In the name of Your son, Jesus, we pray. Amen."

"Amen," I said in unison with everyone else. I wiped my eyes.

Harold looked at me. "Are you okay?"

I nodded. "Yeah, I'm just feeling the Lord's love."

Rhonda unzipped her purse. "Hold on, sis…I mean… what should I call you now?" She handed me a tissue.

"Thanks." I dried my eyes. "And you can call me anything you want."

"Daddy's always gonna be Daddy to me, even though he's really my great-uncle. I've gotta think about all of this. I don't know…"

I smiled. "There's no rush. Whatever you decide is fine with me."

"Is it okay if I call you Granny?" Antoine asked.

"Sure."

Jaimaya rubbed her round belly. "And I guess you're going to be a great-grandma soon…so you're gonna be GG too."

"Did you hear that?" I nudged Harold and smiled. "I'm going to be a great-grandparent. I know I'm too old for you now."

"I think your family is beautiful," Harold said. "And I'm not going anywhere unless you decide to trade *me* in for a younger model."

I laughed. I noticed the elders lining up for their plates, including Sister Sadie.

"Can I get my food now?" Antoine asked.

"Wait until the elders are finished."

Antoine frowned. "It won't be no barbecue left by the time they finish."

"There won't be any barbecue left," I corrected my grandson's grammar.

"Sorry. Any."

"That's much better." I smiled at him. "Don't worry. You'll get plenty."

Jaimaya's cell phone rang. She retrieved it from her purse and looked at the caller I.D. "It's Dad. I've got to take this. Excuse me."

She waddled out of the exit door.

Rhonda turned to Antoine. "Does your father even know you're here?"

He shrugged.

Rhonda frowned. "So you don't know for sure?"

"I don't know, Mom. But I think so."

A minute later, Jaimaya came back to the table. She slowly sat down in her chair.

"Is everything okay?" Rhonda asked.

"Yeah."

"Did you tell Nate that you were bringing Antoine here?"

"Yeah. He knows. Grandpa talked to him."

"He did?"

"Grandpa insisted on having the whole family here today."

"Well, I'm glad he let my baby boy come."

"I'm not a baby, Mom," Antoine declared.

"I know you're not a baby, but you'll always be *my* baby."

Jaimaya touched Rhonda's arm. "You should call him. He's tired of talking through the lawyers."

"He's got my number. He should call me if he really wants to talk."

"He took the first step by letting me bring Antoine today so now, he's waiting for you to take the next step and call him."

"You don't think I tried calling him a million times before I hired Attorney Reed? I don't have any energy for games right now. All I want to do is be there for you and your brother and I won't let anything or anybody get in the way of that. Never again." I paused. "How is he anyway?"

"Call him and ask him that yourself."

Daddy and Sister Sadie came back to the table with their plates. I noticed that Sister Sadie had plenty of vegetables and no chicken.

"You're going vegetarian?" I asked.

She sat down. "I can't help if I don't care for Sister Maple's barbecue."

"That just leaves more for the rest of us." Daddy sat down. "I love my congregation, but God bless them, they sure can tear up some chicken! Y'all should get in line."

"Okay!" Antoine stood up anxiously.

"Run don't walk!" Rhonda hollered.

He walked to the back of the line.

"Are you hungry?" I turned to Harold. "I think I'll wait for the line to die down a little."

"Yeah, that's fine," he said.

"As long as y'all don't wait too long," Daddy said.

Rhonda turned to Jaimaya. "I'll fix you a plate."

"Thanks, Mom, but I'm pregnant, not helpless."

Daddy chuckled as Jaimaya got in line behind Antoine. "They sure got that Foster appetite honest. Amen."

As soon as Antoine and Rhonda came back to our tables with their delicious-looking plates, Harold stood up.

"So I guess you're hungry after all?" I smiled.

"A brotha can always get down with some barbecue chicken, but there's something more important right now..."

Daddy grinned as Harold got down on one knee and looked up at me. He reached out for my hand. As we gazed into each other's eyes, my heart pounded.

"If you give me the chance, I'd like to spend the rest of my life waking up to that beautiful smile." He pulled out a velvet ring box from behind his back. "Jacqueline Marie Foster, will you marry me?"

"Yes! Absolutely!" I cried happy tears as he slid the diamond ring on my finger. We stood up together and shared a tender kiss.

Rhonda's eyes were watery. "I'm so happy for you!" "Isn't that so romantic, Abe?" Sadie smiled at Daddy. He rose to his feet and said, "Listen up, everybody, I'd like to make an announcement! My daughter, Jackie, just got engaged to her boyfriend, Harold."

Folks applauded for us and offered their "Amens" and "Hallelujahs."

"In today's sermon, you might remember me saying that a young man came to my office and he inspired me to live in my own truth. Well, that young man was Harold. He initially came to ask for my daughter's hand in marriage. These days, a lot of men don't bother to extend that kind of respect, especially considering that my baby girl, well, let's just say she's not quite a baby anymore." A few people chuckled. I couldn't help but smile too. "So while Harold and I were talking, we got into a long conversation about life and family that inspired today's sermon. I knew that he was the husband the Lord sent for her."

***

At the end of the dinner, I put my camera on a tripod and set the automatic timer. When the flash of the camera went off, it captured a beautiful portrait of myself, Rhonda, Harold, Daddy, Antoine, Jaimaya and Sister Sadie.

The next day, I ordered a big print of the photo and I put it in a gold frame. I hung it up on my living room wall. For the first time in my life, I was no longer ashamed of myself or my family. In fact, I felt blessed to have them in my life and I loved them more than I ever thought possible.

Epilogue

I've been married to Harold for a year now. We decided to quit our jobs at Center Stage Studios and open up our own photography and videography company together. We've been blessed with a steady flow of clients and it's such a joy for me to share my creativity with the love of my life. By the way, our honeymoon was amazing. Diane was right. Sanctified lovin' between a husband and wife is incredible!

My relationship with Rhonda has never been better. Oftentimes, we just sit in my living room and talk for hours. No topic is off-limits. There is no place for shame. We haven't healed all of our past wounds yet but every moment we spend together brings us closer to a more peaceful place.

I'm so proud of Rhonda. She has stayed sober and is going to graduate with her nursing degree next year. She finally worked out a custody arrangement with Nate. Now, she sees Antoine on the weekends and on Wednesday nights. She is also doing everything she can to help Jaimaya and her new baby. I'm officially a great-grandmother now. Angela Marie was 7 pounds and 6 ounces at birth and as cute as a button from head to toe. I was so honored when Jaimaya gave her my middle name.

These days, our family is planning for another wedding. Daddy will be walking down the aisle at the age of eighty! I'm so happy for him. I helped Sister Sadie pick out her wedding dress. She decided on a gorgeous gown trimmed with white lace and pearls.

People at church are saying that Daddy and Sister Sadie are living proof that you're never too old to find love. Life has taught me that you're never too old to do anything. At fifty-one years old, I have finally let go of my secrets and I am living my dreams. I am so grateful that God never gave up on me and I will spend the rest of my days devoting myself to Him.

Dedication

To my Aunt D. I love you so much! You are one of the strongest and most generous people I've ever known. I pray that the Lord gives you the strength to overcome your addiction.

Note to Readers

Thank you for taking the time to read *Papa Don't Preach*. As you may know, this is my first Christian fiction novel and I'd be honored to hear your feedback. Please feel free to leave a review or contact me directly on my website at www.SadeMorrison.com